Raw Deal

A COVER-UP TURNS DEADLY

Raw Deal

A COVER-UP TURNS DEADLY

Lee Fishman

TransMedia Press
Philadelphia, PA

Library of Congress Cataloging – Publication Data on File

978-1-7364787-2-1
Ebook 978-1-7364787-0-7

www.leefishman.net

For a Friend

CHAPTER
1

A full moon threw shadows across a landscape of sandy nothingness as two U.S. soldiers staggered around the corner of an enormous white hangar. When the taller, fairer of the two stumbled, his dark-haired mate pulled him upright. "Hang on, buddy. You OK, Joe?"

"Happy birthday to the greatest fucking guy in the universe! You were born December 23, and me, I'm December 27th. What are the odds we'd have birthdays a couple days apart? What's our sign again?"

"Shut up, Joe. You're drunk."

Joe gave his friend a shove, "No, you're drunk."

As Joe's legs buckled again, he struggled to keep himself upright. "Tony, you're a pal."

"Be quiet, I hear someone."

Two helmeted MPs, guns drawn, materialized out of the desert night. "Halt! Identify yourselves."

Tony searched for a spot to hide. But Joe, heedless, slammed drunkenly against the hangar's outer wall. "Yo, help me out here," Joe implored. He smashed his shoulder against a door for the second time. When it burst open,

Joe moved inside but the sign overhead, **Warning – Hazardous Material** stopped Tony cold.

An alarm's blast filled the air as lights flashed onto the white protective gear hanging from the wall. In the glare, Joe rubbed his eyes at the sight of metal thermos-type containers. The MPs moved close to the entrance but stayed outside the space where Joe hunkered down.

"You, soldier, I told you to halt. Put your hands on your head and come out or I'll shoot."

Hands up, Tony stopped dead outside the hangar.

Joe, panicking, jumped behind the door. His weight, hitting the wall, sent one of the canisters to the floor, and it broke open at his feet. The drunken soldier looked down, puzzled by the filmy powder expanding upward into the night air. The second MP, going in after Joe kicked the open canister aside and pulled Joe out into the darkness. "Come on, party boy. Let's go." In the glare of their flashlights, they marched the two men off into the night.

Where was he? Looking around, it took Tony several minutes to get his bearings. His eyes scanned a stark gray wall with a stainless-steel toilet and sink in a corner. His head throbbed, and his mouth was dry and sore. And why did his tongue hurt? Then he remembered biting it when he stumbled.

Jagged fragments of a miserable chain of events from the night before reconstructed themselves in his consciousness. When he'd mentioned his birthday was December 23rd, Joe chimed in saying his was four days later. But whose half-assed idea was it to celebrate? All he could remember was that Joe dug out the unopened bottle of single malt he'd kept in his locker waiting for a special occasion. Tony's contribution was the bottle of tequila; and between them, they got totally wasted. It would have been cool if they'd only stayed in their quarters, but somehow, and he can't remember why, they decided to walk around the base.

A groan emanated from the next bunk.

"Dude, you OK?"

"No, not OK."

"I hear you. I'm hungover too."

Breathing heavily with the effort, Joe tried to rise from the metal cot where he lay. "I feel like shit. I can't catch my…" Staggering to the stainless-steel toilet in the corner, he fell, hitting his head on the metal rim.

Only after Tony dragged him back to the bunk did Joe regain consciousness, doubling over as a coughing fit overwhelmed him. Even as Tony tried to lift him up, he choked and gasped. Once the coughing subsided, Tony curled a pillow into a ball, shoving it under his friend's head. Even then, Joe panted for air.

In a panic, Tony ran to the cell door. Banging with his fist, he cried out, "Medic! I need a medic. This man needs to go to sick bay."

CHAPTER
2

Arranging gifts under the tree, Sandi paused to watch her mother set up three TV trays. "Mom, why don't we eat in the dining room?"

Regina, an apron over her skirt and blouse, smiled and shrugged. The circles under her eyes were a little darker, but other than that Sandi thought her mother looked very much the same as she had when they were growing up. "Since Joe's away and you're at school, your father and I eat in here. It's just a habit we got into. The dining room table's too big for just the two of us."

Regina's expression lightened as she heard her husband walk in through the back door. "There's your father. Help me put everything out. Then we can watch the video."

Sandi followed her mother into the kitchen in time to see her father, Ray turn from his rummage in the refrigerator. His eyes lit up at the sight of her. "Hey, Skeeter, how's my little lawyer?" Once he'd smothered Sandi in a hug, he popped the tab on his beer and took a swig.

Her father's good feeling was short-lived, his smile fading, he turned to his wife. "It's just like I thought. 'Happy

New Year! Here's your unemployment check.' They're closing the plant for two weeks. Nice present, huh?"

Regina smoothed wrinkles from his shirt. "We knew it might happen, but let's not think about it now. Sandi's here. Let's eat."

With their plates filled; the family got comfortable. Ray popped in a CD and sat back, riveted by the glow of the TV screen, as an image of a soldier in desert camouflage appeared next to a palm tree. "Hey, Mom, Dad, Sandi, you just missed it. No snow yet, but Santa just went by on a camel. I'm here with my buddy, Tony."

A second soldier ducked into the frame. Brawny with dark curly hair, Tony waved. "Hi, folks. I feel like I know you. I'm trying to keep this guy out of trouble. Merry Christmas!"

Joe jumped back in focus. "Sandi, how's second year? Email me and let me know how you did with the first part of Donovan's contract law class. My notes for the second half must be around somewhere if Mom hasn't thrown them away yet. Just kidding Mom."

Sandi had a million questions she wanted to ask her brother about law school. But first, she'd find the notes, make a list, and include them in her next email.

Her parents stayed glued to the screen as Joe, blue eyes blazing, gave them a running description of the base. "As you can see, we could use a little color around here. It's all beige. Everything, the sand, the buildings, the vehicles, the uniforms. I swear, sometimes even the chow looks beige to me. I guess I shouldn't complain. There is a swimming pool, even though we haven't gotten a chance to use it yet. They got rid of the tents, and now we have trailers to sleep in. Thank God they're air-conditioned. Not much action to speak of. There was a top-secret delivery the other day. Hush, hush. Not sure what it was, but aside from that, we're just going out on recon, guarding a few palm trees and some aircraft. I guess, come New Year's, we'll be training some of the Saudi troops on the equipment. Anyway, love you guys. Miss you. Sandi, take care of Mom and Dad. Gotta go. Be home soon."

Regina wiped her eyes with her napkin, and Ray drained his beer with a look that said he didn't need looking after. Sandi picked up her empty plate. She patted her mother's shoulder. "Mom, it's just the reserves, he'll be home soon. He's not in Iraq, at least."

"I'll never forgive the recruiter who talked Joe into signing up in the first place," Regina said. "And why didn't he tell us first? If I'd known, I would have tried to talk him out of it."

Ray held up his hand to stop the discussion. "Regina, let's not go over this again. In my day, going into the service was just what you did. I didn't want to go, but I went and it was a learning experience, part good, part bad. But there were benefits. How do you think we bought this house?"

"Mom, you couldn't have stopped him. When it happened, he didn't even mention it. Besides, he was already twenty. He didn't need permission." Although

Sandi didn't say it, she knew why her brother joined. He did it to help them out.

Sandi was sure money worries were what landed Joe in the National Guard. Right before his junior year of college, a buddy convinced him that the government would provide a bonus and scholarship money if they signed up together. That meant borrowing less for tuition. And what was so hard? All they had to do was go to a meeting once a month and spend two weeks training in the summer. How could it go wrong? Who could predict everything that followed in the early years of the twenty-first century? That 9/11, the Iraq war, ISIS, and all the other terrorist activity in the Middle East would turn everything upside down? Who could predict that the military, low on recruits, would call up the National Guard sending them off to God knows where. But that's what happened.

"Sandi, take care of Mom and Dad," he'd told her. That was a switch. When he said it, Sandi had nodded back at the screen, even though it was something she'd never thought much about. She'd always counted on Joe to look out for her and her parents. Now, she silently promised to do whatever she could, never thinking of how that might change. She hadn't said anything out loud, but she knew she needed to live up to her word.

How many times had the teachers at Cardinal Preston High asked, "Oh, are you Joe's sister? With that light brown hair and those hazel eyes, you two look a lot alike." Often, she would smile and nod, feeling proud. Still, at school and even at home, she always felt pressured to keep up. Though her parents never said a word, Sandi often wondered if things would have been different if she had been born first instead of Joe. Still, she was the second in her family to finish college, and now she was determined to be the second lawyer, as well. Before he'd left Joe teased her about the two of them setting up an office, calling it Brennan and Brennan, Attorneys at Law. She wanted to believe him anyway even if he wasn't serious about it.

Sandi made her way across the backyard to the converted garage that Joe once laughingly called his office. As the lights flickered on, they illuminated a shrine to the high school careers of both Sandi and her older brother. He'd played football and starred on the debate team. She ran track and was a cheerleader. Digging through the filing cabinet where Joe stashed his notes from law school, Sandi promised herself she would catch up. She planned to be close to finishing her law degree by the time he came home.

She dug out Joe's law school notes, praying they would come in handy. Second semester was about to begin, and if it was anything like the fall of her second year, they'd be pouring on the work. Sandi knew she should call her mom more, and try to get home more on weekends. But God, it was so hard. She'd given some thought to law review but she'd reached a point where she was scrambling just to keep up with what she already had on her plate.

She felt more than a little guilty. Now here was Dad getting laid off, even if it was just until after New Years.

That wasn't so unusual. It had happened before. Year-end was always a slow time at the plant. But things were changing. Companies moved their factories to Mexico and China, where people worked for cheap.

Sandi thought of Janey, her best friend from junior high. When the big steel mill closed down, Janey's family packed up, sold their house, and left town, moving to Texas so Janey's dad could work in the oil fields.

Sandi's guilt twisted her heart. Mom and Dad put every spare nickel they had into their kids, into making their lives better. She didn't think they would stop now. Once she finished law school and got a job, there would be student loans to repay, but she still had big plans to send her folks on a kick-ass vacation, and maybe help them fix up the house. Or maybe she and Joe could convince them to get a new place. Sandi shook her head, knowing that would never happen. Her parents were happy to stay in the house they'd lived in for the past twenty-some years down the street from family and not far from the people they'd known pretty much all their lives.

Christmas came and went, and it was fun to spend a few hours with the relatives, watching the antics of her little cousins and what they made of their mounds of toys. But soon after the twenty-fifth, a wave of boredom, resignation, and gloom washed over Sandi. She tried to brush it away, glad she didn't live here anymore. Would she move back once school was finished? Not if she could help it. What about her friends? If this is what they wanted, then God bless, that was fine. But Sandi wanted something different. And if that meant starting over in a new place, she would do it. Her parents seemed hurt that Sandi was going back before New Year's, but she told them she wanted to get a head start on her studies and look for a part-time job.

Driving back to the city, Sandi ran through the financial tally she knew by heart. There was the twelve thousand she still owed for her undergraduate tuition and now the thirty thousand from her first year of law school.

Sandi pulled Joe's old gray Volvo into the closest parking space she could find and turned on her blinkers. Praying there was no meter maid around, she'd drop off her stuff at the apartment and then go look for a space. She wondered if that spot down by the underpass was legal. If she was lucky, it would still be there. That was one good thing about her parents' neighborhood, you could always find a place to park. Here in Philadelphia, it was survival of the fittest. Still, she was happy for the use of Joe's car. It would make things easier until he got back. Having the car would also help her keep one of her New Year's resolutions. She'd promised herself to go home at least twice a month. It was only a half-hour drive. Hell, it wasn't like they lived on the moon or something.

Finding her house keys, Sandi smiled at the sight of four-year-old Emily knocking on the window and waving to her. She was Sandi's biggest helper. As Sandi backed her way into the front door, Emily's twenty-something mother,

Janine, stuck her head into the hallway. "Hey, girlfriend, looks like you made out like a bandit. Need help?"

Sandi grinned, "No, I'm cool. Let me just run this stuff upstairs. Can you keep an eye on the car for me in case the Parking Authority shows up?"

"Sure. Any chance you could watch Em tonight for a few hours? I have a chance for a gig at the Moonstone."

"I think so. Let me get settled and I'll be right back."

CHAPTER
3

With slow resignation, Regina picked the ornaments from the tree, wrapping them, one by one, in tissue. With the New Year beginning, she was more than ready to move on, thinking ahead, ready to face whatever the month of January had in store.

This year she was afraid she knew. Ray had attended the union meeting the night before. Word at the plant was that they would be cutting back hours and in six months the plant would be closing for good. Operations would move one division to Tennessee and the other division would go to Mexico. Anyone in appliances was welcome to relocate to Tennessee if they wanted to re-apply for their job there. But Ray's parts division was moving below the border to Juarez, Mexico, so, there would be no chance of keeping the job.

Ray brought home a stark message from the union meeting. "This is a plan to get rid of the union jobs." And what could they do? The company claimed a slowdown in orders, fearing stock prices might plummet if profits didn't stay firm. "They care about the stock price and the shareholders," he said. "What about the workers? Not one word about that."

Regina was glad that she had her administrative job at the school district office. There was no chance of that ending anytime soon. She could switch Ray over to her health insurance benefits but what about paying the bills? And what about retirement? They weren't getting any younger. They weren't as bad off as a lot of people. They had a little something saved up. But jobs were scarce. Ray was only fifty-seven. There was talk about the company offering early retirement for people who had their twenty years in and Ray qualified for that. Still, she knew he was too young to sit around the house and watch TV.

Regina heard footsteps on the porch. As the doorbell sounded, she squinted, trying to make out two dark shapes behind the milky glass.

On opening the door to the two men in military dress, Regina's heart stopped. She clutched her chest. An inner voice told her to slam the door in their faces and run in the opposite direction. This wasn't real; it wasn't happening. "No, Joe, NO."

"Mrs. Brennan?" a man wearing captain's bars asked gently.

Regina nodded, starting to crumble.

"May we come in ma'am? I'm Captain Donnelly and this is Chaplain Summers."

As they moved into the living room, Regina took deep breaths, trying to regain her composure.

"Ma'am, perhaps you'd like to sit down. I'm sorry to tell you that your son, Joseph Brennan was killed in an accident. The vehicle he was driving flipped over in a ditch and caught fire. He died bravely trying to save others. The United States Government thanks you for his service."

Dressed in their wintry best, the men commandeered the front porch. Despite the sun's fading rays and the chill in the air, the men stood without coats or gloves. Ray, finishing his smoke, laid a hand on the burly arm of the man closest to him. "Come inside, Art. The coffee's hot and there's something a little stronger if you need warming up."

As Ray moved toward the door, his eyes took in a black town car pulling to the curb. He paused then and turned. The car's rear door opened and Ray headed to the sidewalk to greet the new arrivals.

"Mayor, gentlemen. It's so good of you to be here." Ray's welcoming words were reflected in the silent nods of the onlookers. The men standing on the porch parted silently for the newcomers.

Mayor Tom Creighton shook Ray's hand. "We thought the world of Joe. He had a great future ahead of him"

"Regina's inside. I know she'll want to see you." Ray ushered the men indoors where friends and family clustered around Regina as though offering her a wall of protection against the sorrow waiting to envelop her. Looking up in surprise, Regina took a step forward. "Mayor, thank you for coming."

"Regina, the VFW wanted you and Ray to have this," the mayor said. Stepping aside, he made way for his assistant to come forward; the young man proffering an encased American flag, folded in a triangle.

Looking at it with dull eyes, she tried to respond with an appropriate gesture. "Coming from you Mayor, this means a lot." But her words were swallowed up in the silence surrounding her. As the mayor enfolded her in a hug, Regina's tears flowed.

Taking the handkerchief her daughter offered, Regina turned away. Quickly, Sandi moved toward their guests, "Mayor, gentlemen. Let me get you something to drink."

Following Sandi across the room, the mayor pointed to a framed photograph on the mantel. "See that shot of Joe and me? I think it was taken the day before my election. Joe worked like crazy on my campaign. When it came to politics, he was a natural. We even talked about him running for the state legislature next year."

The two men nodded and Sandi looked at them quizzically. "Where are my manners?" the mayor asked. "Sandi, have you met Len Krause?"

Sandi paused in filling the coffee cups and turned to the newcomer, her face lighting up with a smile. "No, but I heard Joe mention your name many times."

"Joe interned for us that summer after his first year in law school. Hope he didn't bad-mouth me too much. We worked him pretty hard as I recall."

"No way! Joe said working with you was like enrolling in a class called Real World 101."

"Thanks, good to hear. I heard about you too," Krause said. "Do you have the Brennan family talent for hard work?"

Sandi laughed despite herself. "I don't know about that but, Joe inspired me to follow in his footsteps. I'm in my second year at Temple Law. We used to joke about opening an office together."

From behind Len, a dark-haired younger man stepped forward. "Dave Nielsen. Sorry for your loss."

"Before he got called up by the National Guard, the mayor was trying to encourage your brother to run for the state legislature," Len said. "But, to be honest, we had hopes that Joe would join our firm instead, right Dave?"

Dave nodded in agreement as he looked at Sandi. "Did you say you're in your second year?"

Sandi's eyes welled. She looked down as the tears threatened.

Len and Dave's eyes met and Len dug in a pocket. "Here's my card." He handed it to Sandi.

"I know now is not a good time to talk about it but, we could use some help at the office. Some challenging cases are coming up, in case you might be interested."

CHAPTER
4

In the glare of fluorescent lighting, Mark Ricklin emerged wearily from the glassed-in workroom. Over the door, bold signage read, **Decontamination Chamber, Hazmat Gear Required**. Disposing of the day's protective suiting, he nodded to his assistant, "Ready to call it a night?"

"Sounds good to me but I think we may not be done yet." The assistant looked over at the two men standing at the window of the observation room. One was wearing a suit, the other, a shirt with a security badge on the chest. "Isn't that our boss?"

Ricklin groaned. Trying to put a brave face on it, he waved to the man in the suit who stood motionless, not returning the greeting. Ricklin pressed a button and talked into a nearby intercom. "Ken, give me a few minutes to finish clean-up and I'll be right there."

Minutes later, Ricklin strode hurriedly toward the new arrivals. "Ken Daly, always a pleasure. To what do we owe the honor?"

With no prologue, Daly got right to the point. "Give your keys to the security guard," he said with a nod to the man next to him. "Your replacement starts tomorrow."

Ricklin's face caved in. "Ken, I know we've had some issues here but…"

"Issues? That's an understatement."

"But Ken, it wasn't me. You know I've been trying. We were trying to meet the deadline. Unless we shut everything down and start all over, there was no way to meet the Army's vaccine contract. The memo I sent called for increased lab protocols. The budget called for more protective…"

"I don't want to hear it. This was your screw-up. The way this lab's been operating puts our whole company at risk. If the DOD wasn't taking a pause on their vaccination schedule there'd be a world-class stink by now."

"Does this mean I'm fired?"

"Fired? No, at Vectelon, we take care of our people. We found another spot for you. It's out on top of Mount Nowhere but I think you'll like the view."

His superior gone; Mark walked back along the glassed-in wall that separated the lab where the work was done from the animal cages. With his phone, he recorded images of several sick animals, hunched over and lethargic.

Two days later, Mark stood behind another glass-enclosed wall. This time the facility was a small warehouse attached to a much smaller lab. As a young man entered bearing a clipboard Mark looked up from the box he was filling with office supplies and personal effects.

"Boss, the shipment of test tubes just came in. Can you sign?"

"Call Ken Daly." He knocked the clipboard to the floor. "Ask him to sign for it. I'm outta here." The underling raised his eyebrows as Ricklin picked up his box and walked out.

Flashes of red and blue illuminated the night highway. Flashlight in hand, one cop approached the driver's side of the stopped vehicle, a white sedan with Virginia plates. Another New Jersey State police car arrived for backup.

The driver rolled down his window and stuck his head out. Forty-ish, wearing glasses and looking totally professorial, Ricklin asked, "There a problem, Officer? I don't think I was doing more than fifty."

"Pop your trunk."

"What? Is this some kind of weird stop-and-frisk action?"

"You heard me."

The driver pushed a button and the trunk lifted. A second trooper walked around to the rear of the vehicle. Throwing back a tarpaulin that covered the payload inside he let out a long low whistle. "Bingo, here's a live one!" Walking back to the first cop, he held up a brick of white material wrapped in plastic. "There's a whole trunk full of this. Looks like meth."

Mark's face crumbled as they pulled him out of the car and handcuffed him. "Hey, Soccer Dad. What gives? You run out of money for your golf club membership?"

"I don't need your comments. Let's get this over with. I want to call my lawyer."

Minutes later, Mark was perp-walked into a low one-story New Jersey State Police barracks off the turnpike. The first cop led him down the beige cinder block hallway into an equally beige interrogation room with a standard metal-edged table and four government-issue chairs. The trooper deposited Mark at the table. "Why don't you relax for a few minutes and we'll be back to take your statement."

Cornered, Mark snarled, "I'm not making any statement. Like I said, I want to talk to my lawyer."

The second trooper arrived, carrying a telephone. After plugging it into the wall jack, he released the handcuffs from Mark's wrists, telling him, "You've got five minutes."

Mark dug into his wallet and produced a card. He quickly punched in numbers. "Len, it's me, Mark, Mark Ricklin. As soon as you get this message, I need you to get back in touch with me." Putting his hand over the receiver, he looked up asking, "Where am I?"

"You're at the State barracks off Exit 7. Near Edison."

"I'm being held at the New Jersey State Police barracks near Edison." Mark looked at a card the State cop pushed toward him. "Here's the number. 609-891-8176. I need you to get back to me. It's urgent."

The state trooper unplugged the phone. "I guess you'll be joining us for the evening." He signaled for the prisoner to stand.

The two troopers, one on either side, led Mark Ricklin down the hall.

CHAPTER
5

Len steered the silver Porsche off the expressway and onto the exit ramp. The calendar said January but according to the temperature that flashed neon atop the energy company's sign on the 32nd floor, the temperature was a spring-like 55 degrees. "Guess we can thank global warning for today's weather," Len muttered to himself.

It was early. Traffic was still light on the Parkway. Len's favorite route into the city was a broad expanse of boulevard designed to emulate the Champs Elysée. Not a bad way to start the day. This wasn't Paris, but he loved Philly just as much. He glimpsed the Art Museum on his left as he flew toward City Hall before hitting the light that slowed traffic at Logan Circle. Downshifting, he let the roar of the engine fill his ears as he turned south.

He pulled into the parking lot and slowed as Juan, the parking lot attendant, looked at his watch. Pointing to the clock on the wall. It read 7:05. "Dude, you're late"

"I know. I gave myself a little extra time with my new car. You like?"

Tapping his chest, Juan smiled as he pointed to the car's hood. "I'm in love."

Len laughed. Leaning across the leather seat, he opened the passenger side door.

Juan slid in. "Let me show you to my special spot," he said. "Nobody will bother this little honey and I can keep an eye on her for you."

They roared up to the next level.

Sandi locked the door of her second-floor apartment. Giving her appearance a quick check in the hall mirror, she ran a comb through her long fair hair, tucking a stray wisp behind her ears. "Good to go," she told herself as she headed down the front steps of the three-story brownstone and out to the street. She waited there on the corner and once the light changed, she made her way across the lanes of stopped traffic. Shielding her eyes from the glare of the morning sun, she headed south joining the throng of pedestrians heading into the heart of the city.

Fifteen minutes later, she was surrounded on all sides by several tall, glass-sheathed edifices each vying for attention. Looking for an address, she squinted, her eyes moving back and forth from one building to another. Pulling a card from her pocket, she confirmed that the building in front of her was where she wanted to go.

Making her way inside, she stopped to read the company directory on the wall. Finding the correct floor, she joined the throng of workers crowding into the elevators. Getting off at the sixth floor, she looked around the silent carpeted corridor before spotting a polished brass sign next to walnut double doors that read, Krause and Nielsen, Attorneys at Law, LLP.

Inside, she found Len shuffling through papers on the reception desk. When he looked up, surprised, Sandi, fought an urge to turn and run. Did he forget his offer? At the sight of his grin, her fear evaporated.

"Sandi, welcome. Don't mind me. For a minute, I spaced and forgot you were coming in today. How are the folks?"

"Len, thanks for asking. I guess you'd say, it's one day at a time for all of us." She tried to throw off her pain with a smile.

Sandi saw Len's expression change as he realized the sore spot he'd touched. He looked relieved when a woman entered the office. "Wait, here's our office manager. Lorraine, good timing!"

When Lorraine removed her coat, Sandi understood why Len needed help. She looked as though she might give birth any day.

"Lorraine, did I mention that Sandi's starting today? She's going to be helping us out. I know she'll be safe in your capable hands."

"Sandi, great to see you. Let's find a place for your things." Lorraine pointed to a small desk in an out-of-the-way alcove. Dropping her handbag in a drawer, Sandi slipped her coat around the back of the chair.

Just beyond the desk, Lorraine opened a door to a room of tall metal file cabinets where layers of file folders spilled over from the top level. "Not too glamorous for a start but we got a little behind. This morning, why don't you see if you can get these files back in shape."

Inwardly Sandi groaned. *This is what I get for being second-year law?* Plastering on a smile, she nodded as Lorraine left her to the task.

Hours later, Sandi's back ached. Despite the smudge of dust on her cheek, she couldn't help but feel satisfied, knowing that the room was in better shape than when she arrived. The wall clock registered three fifteen. Realizing she'd missed lunch; she settled into a chair for the first time that day. Retrieving a few personal items from her handbag, she arranged them on her desk and sat back as if considering the message on her note card-sized magnet that read: MAKE IT HAPPEN.

Dave Nielsen moved into Sandi's line of vision, seeming to take her presence for granted. "Hi, you know where the photocopier is right?" Without waiting for a response, he continued, "Could you make three sets of these?"

Wordlessly, Sandi held out her hand for the documents and headed back to the file room. Job done; she turned to see Lorraine behind her.

"There you are. Great job, Sandi. Oh, one more thing before I forget."

Considering priorities, Sandi held up a finger. "Let me just get these copies to Dave."

Sandi felt like throwing the papers on the floor and grinding them under her heel but she thought of the tuition bill looming, to say nothing of the rent. So, what if the work sucked? Len agreed to pay her a good hourly rate. Knowing that first days on the job can be rough, she'd just have to bite the bullet, keep her eyes open, and hope for work more in line with her legal aspirations.

"Just let me show you this first. It's right here." Lorraine pointed to the supply closet. "Since you did such a great job on the files, I thought maybe you could give this a try. You might think that lawyers would be neat. I hate to say it, but these guys are slobs." She laughed at her blasphemy.

Later, Sandi closed the door to a tidier closet and slid into her chair just as Len breezed in with a flashy but, well-tailored middle-aged man in tow. He asked with a smile, "How's my lawyer-to-be?"

"Great!" She tried for a confident persona as she waited for the next request to present itself. She's not disappointed.

"Awesome! Can you show Mr. Falcone into the conference room? I'll be right there."

Sandi smiled weakly as she led the client down the hallway to the glass-enclosed conference room. The winter sun was dimming over the tops of the buildings. It would be dark soon.

"Mr. Falcone, may I get you something while you're waiting? Some water, or coffee?"

"No hon, I'm good."

Glad to be out on the sidewalk, Sandi joined the workers' five o'clock parade. On the way home she made a stop at a street vendor and bought some fruit. Her stride on the return trip had lost some of its zip.

Back in the neighborhood, Sandi heard her name as four-year-old Emily called to her from the swing in the little park next to their building.

Encased in a red down jacket, Emily tottered toward her. "Sandi, do you have candy for me?"

Thinking back, Sandi regretted the one time she came home with chocolate kisses and gave one of them to Emily. Since that time, it had become a regular question even when Sandi tried to sidetrack her in another direction. "Guess what? I have something even better for you. Close your eyes."

They stopped at the front stoop while Sandi produced a small tangerine from her bag. "OK, eyes open."

Emily watched, fascinated as Sandi peeled the fruit to reveal jewel-like segments under the orange skin. She offered one to Emily who popped it into her mouth.

Walking over to Sandi, Emily's mother Janine, smiled her thanks. "We're going for pizza. Want to come?"

"Love to, but my feet are toast. My new job seems to be more physical than I expected. I need to crash, and then Ned is coming over so I can help him edit his article for law review."

Sandi blew Emily a kiss. Then as she headed up the steps to the building, Janine called after her, "Don't forget

Friday night. We're playing at the club and my mom's babysitting."

"It's a date."

"Oh, I forgot. A guy came by looking for you this morning. Wanted to return something of yours. Said he'd be back."

"It wasn't Ned, was it? Reddish curly hair, glasses?"

"No, it wasn't Ned. This guy was big, with dark hair, cute, too. Wearing camouflage, almost like a uniform."

CHAPTER
6

A prison guard escorted Len into the gray cinderblock interrogation room. The lawyer fiddled with his briefcase and looked around. Being behind bars still made his flesh crawl, even if it was only for a brief visit. Unbidden, a movie from his youth, ***Scared Straight*** came to mind. If kids only knew what it was like on the inside, they'd think twice before they broke into the candy store for sure.

Len looked up as an orange-clad Mark Ricklin shuffled in, taking a seat across from him. The door slammed shut.

"What were you thinking?"

"It was nothing. A friend asked me to drive a car from New York to D.C. That's all."

"Please…A car that just happened to be filled with crystal meth?"

"I needed some cash, OK? I got kids to feed. I can't get a job since the company put the word out on me. What am I supposed to do?"

Len sighed, trying to quell the annoyance that Mark was stirring up in his chest. "Right, so you're in the car?"

Mark looked over his shoulder at the guard outside. He pulled himself together. "I'm halfway through Jersey. Next thing I know, there's two cop cars behind me. Does that strike you as funny?"

"How fast were you going?"

"I wasn't over the speed limit, I swear."

"That is a little odd."

"More than a little. You've gotta get me outta here."

"I don't know who convinced the judge that you're a flight risk. Let's see if we can get the bail lowered."

"My wife put up the house, but it's not enough."

Somebody's leaning on this guy. Len thought. *But who or why? We don't have a scrap of evidence.*

"Has my friend from Washington called you yet?"

Len shook his head. "Not a word."

Len and Mark Ricklin sat at the defense table. To their right, the prosecutor, smooth and well-tailored stood before the judge.

"Your honor, if I may, this was a huge cache of methamphetamine. I believe it's called 'ice.' It could be worth over two million dollars in street value. Usage in the state is reaching epic proportions."

"Yes, I'm aware of that and in keeping with the Federal Government's 'War on Drugs' initiative, we want to send a message here."

Len stood, "But your honor, my client has no prior record or involvement with the narcotics industry. May

I approach the bench?" At the judge's nod, he stepped forward. "If I may, your honor. We have reason to believe that my client has been arrested in retaliation for a whistleblower complaint that he was about to make."

"Be that as it may, your client was found to be transporting illegal substances. Has your client actually taken steps to file his complaint?"

Len shook his head and stepped back.

"Bail remains at five hundred thousand dollars," the judge said, striking the gavel.

Home from work, Sandi dragged herself up the stairs to her apartment and flipped on the TV. Images of marching, shouting, sign-carrying protestors filled the screen. The national news anchor intoned, "And in Washington today, protestors marched outside the doors of Vectelon's corporate headquarters in protest of the company's supposed plan to sell bio-agents abroad as reported on the Wikileaks website."

Sandi watched for a few minutes and then she got up and went into the tiny kitchen, asking herself, "Am I up for last night's pizza?" Her eye fell on the chart of good foods and bad foods she'd stuck to the refrigerator door. Rummaging in the fridge, she came away nibbling a raw carrot. Remembering to check her landline for messages, she picked up the remote, flicked off the sound on her TV, and grabbed her phone.

"Hey, sweetheart, it's Mom. Call me when you get a chance."

Sandi sighed. The tears fell for several minutes before she got up and walked into the bathroom. Splashing cold water on her face, she looked in the mirror, asking herself, "Why, why?" When no answer came, she filled a glass of water from the tap., gulping it before she returned to the living room, picked up the phone, hitting the speed dial to call home.

"Hi, Mom. How are you doing?" The conversation continued innocuously while both women strived to maintain a brave font.

"The job's fine…it's getting there. They have me doing a lot of basic work until I get the lay of the land. Then, I'm hoping I'll be able to do something a little more challenging. The office manager, Lorraine will be going out on maternity leave early. She's not due for a while but she's having some issues and the doctor is telling her to stay in bed. Who knows when or even if she'll be back anytime soon? The good news is that I'll probably have a job over the summer if I want it. So, that's a no-brainer, of course, I do."

On the other end, Regina broke into sobs.

"Mom, do you want me to come home? I can be there in an hour or so. Where's Dad?"

Regina pulled herself together. "Your father will be home soon. He's been working down at the gas station part-time. I'll be OK. You stay there and do what you have to do. Love you."

"OK, Mom. Love you too."

Hovering over a stack of books on the kitchen table, Sandi opened the top one. With a sigh, she ran her finger over the syllabus for the Commercial Law course that was tucked inside. Grabbing a yellow highlighter, she marked the due date for the next assignment.

Glancing at the calendar on the wall, she tore off the top page and threw it in the trash. "That's it for February," she said. Calculating when she might receive her paycheck, Sandi scribbled a note on the second Friday in March before she returned to the living room. Taking out her laptop, she perched on the edge of the small sofa, logged on, and began to scroll through her notes. Soon her eyes closed and she fell asleep.

Surrounded by a gaggle of reporters, Len walked up the steps of the courthouse. "Let's talk later, guys. I don't want to keep the judge waiting." He shook hands and waved.

At the top of the steps his partner, Dave, intercepted him and they hurried inside. "For once, could you just not play to the grandstand?"

"Don't worry about it. I know how to handle this. What's the schedule look like?"

"The jury's on their way back."

At the courtroom door, Len adjusted his suit and slicked back his hair before he and Dave ushered their client, Frankie Falcone, down the aisle. Onlookers gave Falcone the high sign in support. As the attorneys took their seats, Len gave a nod to the bailiff.

At a signal, the paneled door opened, and the judge, Anita McDonald, strode into the courtroom. The bailiff intoned, "All rise for Judge McDonald."

The judge took her seat. The bailiff whispered in her ear, and she nodded. A door opened to the right and the jury filed back into the courtroom.

Len gave Dave a look and a nod when he noticed that most of the jury members were looking in their direction, always a god sign. He leaned behind the defendant to brush an imaginary piece of lint off his client's well-tailored back.

There was a buzz in the rear of the room and the judge waited for quiet to be restored. "Ladies and gentlemen of the jury have you reached a verdict?"

The jury foreman stood, intoning, "Yes, your honor."

"Will the defendant please rise?'

Falcone stood, as Dave urged him forward.

"Mr. Foreman, how do you find?"

"We find the defendant, Francis Falcone, not guilty of all charges."

A roar of approval erupted from the courtroom. Len slapped his defendant on the back and they shook hands all around. Falcone's wife, a flashy blond in an expensive navy suit, leaned over to plant a kiss on Len's cheek. The only unhappy face is that of the prosecutor who gathered up her paperwork in silence. She stopped to speak to her assistant and then stood back as the victorious contingent processed up the aisle.

Outside, reporters mobbed Len while Dave stood off to the side with a hint of a frown.

"Len, Len. Were you worried about the verdict?"

Len slapped Falcone on the back. "Not really, I knew we had a strong case. There was very little evidence against my client."

Falcone piped up. "Len Krause is a scholar and a gentleman. And now we're gonna go celebrate. Youse are all invited."

The reporters broke into a laugh. Len walked over to Dave. "Are you coming?"

"I'll pass. You know how I feel about this guy. To be honest with you, he makes me sick." Dave walked off in one direction and Len, Falcone, and a slew of followers headed off in another.

CHAPTER
7

When she was a kid, this was the kind of Saturday Sandi loved. She sat at the window, watching as the fat snowflakes fell softly, landing on the bare branches of the tree. Back then, she would have already been outside, rolling around in it, making snow angels, and hoping for enough snowfall to make a snow fort in the backyard.

It was different in the city. The pristine white surface only lasted for maybe an hour until traffic and the other intrusions of urban life turned the snow from white to gray, then to slush.

Sandi pried her eyes from the window and tried to force herself back to the books. She could have used some help with the focus. This semester was so different. Would she be able to get through it with her average intact? Maybe she should just have taken the semester off like her mother suggested. But no. If she did that, then the second semester of the courses she'd already taken that fall would have to wait a whole year. By then, who knew how things would stand? No, she didn't feel like there was any choice.

The sound of the buzzer was a welcome intrusion. Looking down to the street, she couldn't see who was there. All that was visible was the top of someone's head. "Look up," she silently commanded. But whoever it was didn't seem to be getting her mental communication. She went to the intercom. "Who is it?"

"I'm looking for Sandi. Is that you?"

"And you are?"

"I'm a friend of your brother. I have something for you. May I come up?"

Sandi remembered Janine's message and she buzzed him up. "Second floor, OK?"

She opened the door to a dark-haired, handsome thirty-something guy. He was dressed in a mismatched combination of fatigues with a down vest thrown over a flannel shirt. Not overly tall, yet with arms bulging through shirtsleeves, the man before her had a physical command of his space.

"Now I recognize you from the video Joe sent. It's Tony, right? Come in."

Minutes later they were seated next to each other, with Sandi holding a book, ***To Kill a Mockingbird***, as though there might be a message between its pages. Later she would realize that what she held in her hands was the last and most direct link to her brother. Before he gave it to Tony, Joe must have held the book, and now it was back with her. Shaking the thought away, she tried to focus on what he was saying to her.

"When I saw your name in it, I thought you'd want to have it back."

"But how did you…?"

"How did I have it? Joe loaned it to me. He couldn't believe I'd never read it before. Have to admit that reading has never been my strong suit. But I liked it."

"I gave it to him as a birthday present. It was one of his favorites."

"I'm so sorry. It should have been in the rest of Joe's things when they sent them back to the family. But it got stuffed down in my gear. It was only after I got back that I found it."

"Are you out now? Out of the service, I mean?"

Tony nodded before looking away.

Sandi opened the back cover of the book, and a photo fell out. Tony picked up the photo and handed it back. It was a picture of her and Joe holding up a sign that read, "Brennan and Brennan." Sandi reflected on it for a few seconds. "It was our little joke," she said, turning away as the tears flowed.

"Can I get you some water?"

Shaking her head, Sandi reached for a tissue. "When they came and told Mom about the Humvee accident, our whole family fell apart."

"Humvee accident?" Tony's voice was incredulous.

"Didn't you know? His Humvee ran over a landmine."

"I wasn't there when Joe passed away. They'd sent out our unit on patrol, but…"

"What happened? What did you hear?"

"I'm sorry. A lot of stuff is classified."

"What do you mean classified?"

"Sorry, I don't want to keep you." Tony stood and turned toward the door. "It looks like the weather's getting pretty nasty out there."

Sandi followed, putting a hand on his arm. "Can we keep in touch? Where are you staying?"

Rummaging in his pocket, Tony pulled out a scrap of paper. Accepting the ballpoint Sandi offered, he scribbled a number and handed her the slip of paper. "You can leave a message for me at this number. It's the Vet's Center. I'm from out of state, but I plan to hang out here for a while, and help out some of the guys with a project we're working on."

"Were you and Joe in the same unit?"

"We were until I got transferred. That was after Joe got sick."

"Sick? But we never heard anything about that."

He headed to the door, then turned back to give Sandi a quick hug. "I'm glad I finally got to meet you. It feels good to talk about Joe."

After Tony left, Sandi had so many questions, too many. Was that what made him leave so quickly? Only after he was out the door did Sandi stop and wonder how he'd found her, but it was too late to ask. She hoped she might have a chance the next time they met if there was a next time. She picked up the photo again, turning it over to read what was written there. "Ain't no stopping us now. Brennan and Brennan set to open when you graduate in '08."

Sandi knew she should study, but how could she concentrate? She paced the room and came to rest at the window, nose pressed against the glass. Transfixed by the falling snowflakes, she stood silent. A tear ran down her nose, and she wiped it away with the back of her hand. How could there be so many tears still be left to cry? It seemed like she must already have shed them all. But it wasn't just the tears. Eventually, they would dry. No, it was the realization that the hole that opened up in her life would stay fresh and sore, a wound that wouldn't heal for a long time to come.

Sandi fought with herself. She lifted the phone from its cradle several times throughout the evening. Should she call her parents, tell them about Tony and what he'd said? Should she ask Len about what to do with the information? Would he have any suggestions? He knew Joe. It wasn't like they didn't share a history. What she needed were facts. Isn't that what the professors at law school always stressed? Chase down the facts and get to the truth.

As Len dashed by the reception desk, Sandi looked up from where she sat reading ***Legal Practice, 9th Edition***. "I see they're still using that old chestnut," he said.

"Afraid so. Lorraine told me you were Temple Law, too. I wondered if we had any of the same professors?"

Len shook his head. "Doubt it. It's been a while. Who's teaching Criminal these days?"

The ringing telephone cut off Sandi's response. "Good morning, Krause and Nielsen."

Len moved past and headed down the corridor.

"Mr. Krause, I'll see if he's in. May I have your name, please?"

Len paused at his door and mouthed, "Who?"

Sandi put her hand over the receiver, "Says she's a friend of Mark's. Shall I take a message?"

"No, I'll take it." He headed into his office and shut the door.

CHAPTER
8

Greta Peterson woke up with a cottony taste in her mouth. She hadn't planned on having more than one drink when she got home from work, but somehow, she'd downed two-thirds of a bottle of burgundy just to calm her nerves. Life had taken a turn she hadn't expected.

How had she arrived at the spot where she now found herself? Like so many other ambitious young lawyers of her generation, she was drawn to Washington. And where better to find the career of her dreams than in Congress? Not that she had any ambitions to run for public office. According to her Myers Briggs personality profile, she was more of a behind-the-scenes type, more of a nerd who loved researching all the details. And she was good at it too, or so her boss and mentor, Charley Gross had told her on more than one occasion. And as chief of staff for Congressman Bergson of California, Charley should know.

Was she what they called a 'policy wonk?' Maybe so. In some circles that was considered a badge of honor. When Bergson retired, Charley left Capitol Hill and went to work for the Lombard Global Lobbying Group, taking

Greta with him. They worked closely, and every day it was something exciting. You never knew who you might meet. Somehow, though, she'd lost the thread. It started when Charley decided to go back to his home state of Michigan to run for office. Sadly, he hadn't asked her to come along for the ride.

The high fees Charley brought in had made life easy for her and the rest of his consulting team, but her mentor was no longer there. She took a look at her life, then, and decided a change was called for.

What was she doing? She was tired of living in cramped D.C. apartments. At thirty-three, it was time for her to have a place of her own.

With those high-flying days behind her, she'd taken a job as inside counsel at Vectelon. These days she was more than a little embarrassed to tell people that she worked for a defense contractor. But she'd needed the money, and the pay was good. She'd tried to pass the company off as a conglomerate, mentioning some of their non-military operations. She told herself she'd only stay there long enough to get a down payment on a house together. Then she'd look for another job, something a little closer to her own values.

With real estate in the D.C. area so damned pricey, saving up took longer than she'd planned. Time passed and then she found it, the place she'd been looking for. It was small, with two bedrooms, and one and a half baths, but it had so much charm, and the cutest little postage stamp of a garden out back. And those blue shutters and the persimmon orange door just grabbed at her heart. Even though it cost more than she planned to pay it felt like what she needed.

To begin with, the day hadn't started well. That morning on her way into the Vectelon building, she'd been puzzled by all the people out on the sidewalk, carrying signs and shouting through bullhorns. She squinted at a few of the women who wore feathers in their hair. Was that a TV camera crew that just pulled up? Stopping the security guard by the door, she asked, "What's going on?"

"We heard it's some tribe from West Virginia. They're here to protest."

"Vectelon is hazardous to the lives of our children," they shouted. "Vectelon must stop the deadly research."

As the day dragged on, the noise level grew. Even on the eighth floor, Greta could hear shouts of protest. When the employees complained that they couldn't get on or out of the lobby door, the D.C. police moved the protestors across the street into the park.

It was a clear night and from the top-floor conference room, she could see the Capitol Building off in the distance. Most people had already cleared out of the building by seven or so, but checking her watch, Greta told herself she'd probably be staying late again tonight. Chris, one of her interns, his face red with effort, wheeled in yet another flatbed piled high with trunks of documents.

"Greta, this is the last of it."

She turned from the shredder and pointed to the stack on the floor. "Let's stack them up here, and then you can help Brendan finish."

Chris did as he was told as a second intern wheeled out the empty cart. Glancing at a stack of papers next to the shredder, Greta pulled a document from the top of the pile and read it before placing it on the ledge by the window. With the two interns engrossed in their shredding duties, she smoothly slid it into a folder, then slipped the folder into her briefcase

Another thirty minutes and the buzz of the shredders fell silent. Greta's boss, Ken Daly, appeared, "OK, guys. Looks like we're done here for now" His words caused the two interns to look up hopefully. "You can go."

"Cool. Thanks, Ken. See you tomorrow."

The two sidled past Daly, their faces mirroring relief before they practically ran to the elevator. As her boss watched them disappear down the hall, Greta took the moment to slide her briefcase out of sight under the table.

With the interns gone; Daly turned back to her. His eyebrows raised, "How much longer?"

"Another hour, I'll check around just to make sure."

Daly grimaces, "It's all got to be gone before the auditors get here, understand?"

"Trust me; it will be."

"Some people would love to make a federal case out of this, like your buddy, Ricklin," Daly said before turning on his heel and moving toward the elevator

Greta's headache was back, and she longed for a drink. But she was glad for the time alone. Ken Daly's bulldog face made her sweat. You didn't have to go far inside his head to know what he was thinking. Her only chance for survival here was that she knew where a few of the bodies were buried. But maybe just a few. With that in mind, she held tight to what she just found, one of the specific documents Daly charged her with destroying.

It felt like it was time to make her escape before the shit all came raining down as she knew it would. She knew she should get her resume back in shape. Maybe she should just bag it all, leave town, and go into public service law, like her cousin who worked for the people of Appalachia.

Vectelon's export license, only temporary, would expire in just days. Before that happened, she was determined to do as Mark asked and send a copy to his lawyer, Len. Maybe another copy should go to the office of the Director of Government Oversight. She'd mentioned that to Mark before, and he'd brushed her off. But by now he must have changed his mind.

She came to Washington to do good. How did she ever get involved with a company like this? It was not long after she started at Vectelon that she and Mark met at a neighborhood softball game. He was on a different team, but they were introduced by a mutual friend who had worked at the same consulting firm as Mark.

She wasn't attracted to him physically, that was for sure. He was such a nerd with his curly hair falling in his eyes and those thick glasses! Still, there was something quirky about him that had attracted her attention. After the game, Greta tagged along when both teams went for beers outside at Barnard's Patio. Turned out it was Quizzo Night, and Mark's team won, hands down, easily blowing the competition out of the water. He had answers for all of it, the bookish stuff, the pop culture, even the sports, all in one package. She'd never met anyone with such a command of facts. Later, when they brought out the mic for karaoke, he recruited her and two others for a rendition of Uptown Girls. And the house went crazy.

A couple of weeks later, she ran into him at the Walmart outside Alexandria and realized that they lived within minutes of each other. They'd exchanged emails, and not long after that, he'd invited her and a date for a barbeque. She met his wife, Rita, and the kids. And she and Mark became friends.

After he walked off the job, her good deeds came back to haunt her. Ken confronted her with an article about some of Vectelon's proprietary information that had turned up on WikiLeaks. Though she couldn't be sure that Mark was responsible, she couldn't blame her boss for being angry. Common sense told her to cut off contact with him. And yet, she admired his daring.

This was getting crazier by the day. Now she was careful never to use her computer, her phone at work, or the landline at home to get in touch with him. Before he was arrested, he'd slipped notes under her door and asked her to respond to him in the same way. She wouldn't do that. What if they were watching his house? A few times she called his cell from a pay phone when she could find one that still worked.

After he left Vectelon, Mark suggested she buy a track phone and throw it away every month. Was Mark delusional? Was he crazy? Sometimes she wasn't sure. He had all these stories that seemed to tie together, but how was that possible? The most shocking was what he told her about Vectelon's connection with a bio-agent program.

After he was arrested, Mark asked Greta to call his lawyer, Len Krause. Mark said he could be trusted. He wasn't anyone she'd ever heard of but when she Googled him, the guy had an interesting history—some high-profile cases. Like a good snoop, she'd researched the other stories Mark told her. First, there was the vaccine. When the DOD sought and secured the FDA's permission to dispense with patients' informed consent, it forced over two million soldiers to accept injections of an experimental anthrax vaccine, a patented product of Vectelon Corp. She remembered Mark's words. "The Nazi doctors were tried at the Nuremberg trials for conducting experiments on powerless subjects without their consent." *Was this any different?* Greta had learned that, courtesy of the Pentagon, the DOD had opted to experiment on their soldiers in the same way.

That wasn't all. Greta remembered Mark wondering aloud if maybe the vaccine Vectelon produced was of "questionable" quality. When Greta asked why, he'd said he'd heard that some of the facilities where it had been manufactured were found to be of substandard condition.

A judge's preliminary injunction halted further sales to the Pentagon. However, since the DOD had already paid for the vaccine, Vectelon was still contractually required to complete the process. Soon after sales of their vaccine were curtailed, the company came back and tried again with other products. This time around, the company looked for a new laboratory facility. Strangely, they set one up on an Indian reservation. When Greta asked why, Mark told her that the reservation, a sovereign entity, was not subject to state laws. Therefore, substances that would have been considered illegal if produced elsewhere could be manufactured there.

With a Ph.D. in microbiology, Mark was brought in to head the cleanup crew. He was responsible for getting this new laboratory up to code. Once he came on board, however, his superiors pushed him to cut corners and move fast. Mark soon learned why. With the vaccine on the back burner, the company planned to produce bio-agents and sell them abroad. After the company pushed him around, he and Greta talked about going public with what he knew about Vectelon's shady dealings. She reminded him that if he did, he would be accusing the company of federal crimes, of conduct that threatened the public safety and welfare.

CHAPTER
9

Dave Nielson put the finishing touches on his PowerPoint, the one he'd be presenting later that day at the Union League. The topic was one he hoped was on the cutting edge, "Deregulation and the Derivatives Industry – Where's it going?" He hoped to attract some attention from the financial services players in town for a convention. True, Philadelphia was a backwater compared to what the high-flyers were doing in New York, but a couple of major banking concerns were still headquartered here. And there were also the accounting firms who were heavily involved with those banking clients. Maybe he could pick up some work from them.

After all, he'd been named one of the Top Forty Lawyers under Forty. To make it happen, he'd lobbied his friend, Sam, who was on the *"forty under forty"* nominating committee for his inclusion on the list. As an added incentive he'd made a generous contribution to Sam's favorite cause, the ACLU. And it had worked. Just barely, he'd told himself with a laugh. He was staring his 39th birthday in the face at the end of next month. Still, he'd finally gotten some recognition, something for his accomplishments, not just work his father had funneled to him or, worse, Len's leftovers.

Now they'd see what he could bring in. He was more than ready to change the firm's tenor of work—time to get away from the low-rent criminal types that Len seemed to favor. While Len called them colorful, Dave referred to them as "garbage" when his partner wasn't around to hear. He wanted corporate work, real business stuff. Sure, he could have gone into one of the bigger firms, and maybe he should have, but now it was too late. Besides, he had to admit that his class ranking in law school was far from the highest.

Like it or not, he'd practically inherited the partnership with Len. It was a marriage of convenience for both of them, and they tried to make the best of it. When his older brother, Len's first partner, wanted to head to Wall Street to work in the financial sector, Dave's father gave him the money to buy out his brother's share of the practice. Even so, Dave got pissed whenever Len joked about saving him money by not having to change the name of the firm on the door.

Dave finished a final run-through of the screens for his presentation and sat back, satisfied. He was good to go. Closing the laptop, he adjusted his tie and hit the breath spray he kept in the drawer. He was ready to meet the prospective client prospect waiting for him out front.

Tall, well-tailored, and healthy-looking, George Hendricks was a member of his father's generation. And if he had to guess, Dave would say he likely played golf at least once a week, and probably left the office every day at five.

It wouldn't be hard to feel good about having a client like George, even if he was his father's old college roommate. He was sociable, knew a lot of people, and could steer some work his way. Dave plastered on a big grin and steered George into the conference room, where they made small talk and traded a couple of golf jokes before Dave asked, "George, how can I help you?"

"How much do you know about the insurance game, Dave?"

Dave thought back to his first summer job working in the mailroom at the local insurance company. "Well, I did some work on a distribution system at Penn Life when they were still operating here."

"What did you think of their operation?"

Dave pictured himself trundling the mail chart through the company's corridors distributing incoming mail, a slightly chubby eighteen-year-old in a blue button-down and chinos. "Seemed solid, but their technology needed updating. As I recall, it seemed a little rudimentary."

"Insurance. It's the best-kept secret in the business world."

Dave laughed, nodding as he sat back to listen.

"People send you piles of cash, and you do your best not to have to pay out claims. That's an inside joke."

Dave laughed appreciatively.

"So, we love the fact that we can now siphon some of our earnings, strike that, let's call it our reserves into this fast-moving stock market. Unfortunately, some of the folks in the state insurance office feel differently, and now we're staring at some possible regulatory problems. Have you worked much in that area, Dave?"

Dave tried to think of some of the financial services lingo from the screens he'd just been memorizing. "Regulations have changed, opened up a lot of opportunity. I'd love to put you together with some of the people I've been working with, hedge fund managers with lots of New York connections," Dave thought of his brother. "Let's see what we can come up with."

George clapped Dave on the back, smiling broadly. "Sounds good, I'll have my secretary send you the file with some numbers."

"Great, we'll look forward to sinking our teeth into the…"

Dave noticed George's attention shift elsewhere as Len strode past the conference room's glass enclosure. Len waved a folder he'd retrieved from his office.

"He looks familiar. Didn't I see him on the news recently?"

Dave had hoped to avoid this moment but with a sigh, he called out, "Len, have you got a second?"

"On my way to court, what's up?"

"Meet our new client, George Hendricks. George, this is my partner, Len Krause."

"Len, your face is familiar."

Dave's smile tightened. "You probably saw him on TV. He was featured in that book, ***Breaking with the Mob***?"

"Yes, I've seen it."

Len seemed pleased but harried. "Ancient history." He looked at his watch. "Great meeting you, George. Our firm looks forward to working with you."

Students clustered in the front row as the professor, a youngish fifty-something, paced back and forth. Sandi looked up from her notes to hang on his every word. "So before you can even piece the case together, you've got to investigate and get the facts. Do you know what I mean by that, Ms. Brennan?"

"Find out what really happened. There's a big difference between the way things are, and the way people say they are."

"Correct. Start with an open mind. Talk to everyone. Listen to their story and then…look for the paper trail." He checked his watch. "Let's end it here. For our next meeting, you'll want to prepare Chapters Six through Nine on documentation methods." Within seconds, Sandi had tossed her books in a bag. Heading out the door, she took off for the subway.

Glad that her class had ended early, Sandi pushed the elevator button for the sixth floor. The lobby clock told her she was only five minutes late, and she hoped no one would notice. The streets were less congested than usual. Today was Good Friday and a lot of offices were closed. It was still early enough that there might not have been any calls. She hoped. Lorraine had a doctor's appointment, and she'd told Sandi she would need to answer the phones until she got back.

Just as she reached the dark wood doors to Krause and Nielsen, Len burst out and grabbed her by the arm. "Sandi, perfect timing. Come with me."

"What about the phones? Lorraine is at the doctor."

"Don't worry, the service will pick up." He ushered her back into the elevator, pushing the button for the ground floor. Out on the street, Len guided Sandi around the corner to the parking lot nearby. Sandi tugged her collar up around her ears as a cold March wind swirled through the dim sunless recesses between the buildings. Len threw Sandi a grin over his shoulder. "How's school? Anything interesting?"

"So far this semester, a little dry. Kind of theoretical. If only I could get my teeth into something real."

"We'll see if we can change that." Len nodded, beckoning her on. They emerged onto the lot's top level. Len steered her toward his Porsche ensconced in solitary splendor off to the side.

Despite the gloom, Sandi's eyes popped in appreciation. "Cool car."

"Thanks, one of these days I'll take you for a spin." He opened the trunk and after digging around, extracted a bulging accordion file. "Here's what I want you to do. Take this back and make two copies of each of the marked pages." He planted the portfolio in Sandi's arms. As though the matter was settled, Len jumped behind the wheel. Sandi forced a grin as he fired up the engine and waved to her before he disappeared down the exit ramp.

Sandi shrugged, hoisted the burden onto her hip, and retraced her steps. Back in the office, she wished she could foist this copying job onto someone else's shoulders but she seemed to be the only one around. There had been some talk of hiring a temp, but that hadn't happened. Lorraine was due to arrive after lunch, but for now, it was just her. Finding a cart, she hauled the stacks of paper into the file room. She was hoping to use the document feeder but, after looking over the files she could see many pages were tabbed and clipped, and needed to be done one by one. Fighting off boredom, she found herself reading the documents as she worked.

"Contractual leasing agreement – the Manoaka Nation, Manoaka, West Virginia agrees to lease 10 acres to Vectelon Corporation for biotechnology product development, testing, and manufacture for five years."

When the phone rang, Sandi stopped to answer it, carefully marking her progress with the seemingly endless task. She answered, modulating her voice in imitation of Lorraine's measured tones. "Krause and Nielsen, how may I help you?"

As she jotted down details of the caller's message, the door opened and the familiar face of her friend, Ned appeared. "Pretty awesome surroundings you've got here, girlfriend. I could get used to this."

"Ooh, Ned. I was just going to call you. but something got pushed on me. I don't think I can go to lunch today. At least not now. I'm not sure when Lorraine's gonna get in, and I'm in charge. Nobody else is here."

"You're breaking my heart. But we're still on for tonight, right?

"Sure, I just have to find out the address where Janine is playing."

"How about I go get us a sandwich for now?"

"Do you mind? I've got about a ton of documents to copy."

"There's a good deli around the corner. What do you want?"

Before Sandi could decide what to order, a man with a brown maintenance uniform entered. "This is Krause and Nielsen, right?"

"Yes, May I help you?"

"Maintenance sent me. Here's the work order." He flashed a clipboard with a pink worksheet attached.

"What is it? Nobody mentioned anything."

"Supposed to check the circuits. Problem with the electrical. Your lines are overloaded. The office next to you is shorting out."

Sandi looked from Ned to the man in brown. "I haven't heard anything about it. Nobody called, and the office manager didn't mention anything."

"Yeah, well, you wanna call the supervisor? Go ahead."

Sandi hated to appear indecisive. "OK, you know where to go?"

With a nod, the man moved past reception, heading into Len's office. Ned frowned at her. "What's up with that?"

As a bike messenger arrived with a package, Sandi signed for it, and the phone rang again. Before picking up, she told Ned, "Get me a corned beef special and a diet coke."

"Back in fifteen."

Sandi's intuition was pricking her. Suddenly remembering that the office next door was empty, she hurtled down the corridor toward the lawyer's office. There she found the maintenance man kneeling on the floor behind Len's desk. Screwdriver in hand, he was replacing the round metal plate under Len's credenza.

"Can I see that work order again?" She reached for the clipboard perched on the ledge.

Maintenance was too quick. He grabbed the clipboard and flipped the pages. "Gee, I'm sorry. Wrong office. They got this screwed up. I better go check with the boss. Have a nice day."

CHAPTER
10

Janine wiped the sweat from her forehead. She took the guitar strap from around her neck and gently tucked her instrument into a protected corner behind the amp. One of her bandmates, Jack, a short, bearded drummer, hugged her. Exhilarated and glowing, she grabbed the water bottle perched next to her on the keyboard and guzzled half of it without taking a breath.

Stepping off the stage, she joined her friends at their table. Ned gazed at her in amazement. "Janine, who knew you were such a house on fire? Your band is raucous!"

Sandi elbowed him in the ribs. "Why did you doubt it? I told you she was amazing. This chick can rock!"

Janine cracked up. "It's about time you two bookworms came out. I've only been trying to get Sandi here, for what, the last three months? You guys are overdue for a little fun."

"Yeah, sorry if I've been a drag. Since I talked to Tony, I have been down. It's confusing."

Ned gave Sandi a comforting hug. "That will all be there waiting for you to think about tomorrow. But for right now, let's party. Ladies, what can I get you to drink?"

Monday morning, Sandi was back on telephone duty. "Good morning, Krause and Nielsen. How can I help you?"

Sandi put the caller on hold and called out toward Len's open door, "Len, it's George Hendricks. Are you in?"

Sandi was oblivious to Dave, who stopped in his tracks, mid-corridor, coffee cup in hand. His face reddened in anger.

"Yeah, I'll take it." Not sure who the caller was, he picked up; his voice uncertain. "This is Len Krause."

Seeing Dave's expression, Sandi squinted at the words on the computer, feigning interest in the document on the screen in front of her.

Hovering at Len's door, Dave listened in on the conversation. At the goodbye, he charged in. "What the hell was that about?"

Len looked up and sighed. "That was George Hendricks."

"Yes, I know who it was. Why did he call you?"

Len's voice expressed his consternation. "He says he wants me out front on the IRS negotiations or if his case goes to trial. I told him I'd talk it over with you."

Dave picked up a book on the desk as if to throw it then stopped himself. "Hendricks is my client. I brought him in."

"Don't take it personally. I tried to talk him out of it. But, you heard, he was insistent."

"You steal my client and I shouldn't take it personally?"

"Isn't it more important to keep the business in the firm? Let's not make a big deal over who handles what. There's more than enough work for the two of us. We'll both make money on it."

Dave had been looking forward to his racquetball date with Sam. It had been on his calendar for over a week and it gave him a good excuse to leave. He'd slammed out of the office and got to the club early, working off some steam before Sam arrived.

Punching the bag, he imagined Len's face in front of his eyes. Then suddenly, without his even realizing it, the face morphed into that of his father, and he hit the bag all the harder remembering all the times when it had been his older brother who was the star in the family constellation. The anger wore him out, and he gulped a sports drink, hoping it would revive his momentum. His energy level sagged, but there was still plenty of pent-up anger and he hoped it wouldn't throw his game off. Just as he checked his watch, Sam bounded onto the court, looking fit.

"Hey Dude, ready to play? I'm feeling energized. Don't know about you, but I had a great day."

Usually, Dave could expect to beat Sam at least part of the time. But not today. He felt drained. On Sam's last serve, he missed what should have been an easy shot, slipped, and fell to the floor of the court. Sam looked on in consternation as Dave picked himself up and stalked from the court.

"Easy, easy there, guy. What's bugging you?" Sam picked up the racquet and followed Dave. "C'mon, let's finish the game. These courts aren't easy to book. I hate to waste the time."

"This club sucks. I'm telling the manager if he doesn't resurface this fucking court, he'll have one less member on the books.

"Forget it. You're just having an off day," Sam said as he made a mime of looking at his watch. "Maybe I'll just skip the steam room and try to make the seven-fifteen train."

"What's the rush?" Forced to acknowledge his culpability in screwing up their evening, Dave winced at the edgy sound of his own voice. "Don't you want to go for a drink, at least?"

"Not this week." Sam was already opening his locker. "Got that trial coming up, the one I was telling you about. Securities fraud."

Dave sighed. "Securities fraud, now that would be a relief. Drug dealers, mobsters, whistle-blowers. These are the clients that parade through our doors."

Sam opened his locker, changed, and stuffed his gym clothes into a bulging briefcase. "Do they pay their bills?"

"Yeah, in cash."

Sam laughed. "So, what's the problem? Len's a money machine. Relax, you've got it made. Coast a little."

Dave knew he should keep it light, and he tried to smile, but he could still feel the muscles in his neck contract. "I don't feel like coasting. I want out. His dirtbag clients make me want to puke."

"You want to be a rainmaker? OK, have it your way." Sam's voice let Dave know that he was losing interest. "Make your own contacts." Sam closed his locker. "Talk later."

Yesterday had been Lorraine's last day. Before she left, Lorraine told Sandi, "I'm not taking any chances with this one." After suffering a miscarriage two years before, Lorraine was advised by her doctor to get in bed and stay off her feet. And she was following his advice.

On her way out the door, she'd handed Sandi the keys to the office and wrote down her home number and her personal e-mail. "You can call me if you need to. I'll be home."

Sandi would be doing the work of two people even though she had only signed on to work twenty hours a week. Still, when Len hinted at a raise, she'd assured him she could do more. And, of course, she could always use the extra money. This semester, most of her classes were at night anyway.

Even so, she felt relieved when Len told her, "If you need it, take some time off." She planned to take him up on it so as not to miss the one morning class on her schedule. Still, she was glad when Len said if things got too busy, maybe they could hire a temp.

Len poked his head in. "Here's a golden opportunity to show what you can do. Are you up for a challenge?"

Sandi hit the pause button on the copier with relief. "Really? Do you mean it?"

"Sure. Start with a Lexis search on Mark Ricklin for the last ten years. News articles, lawsuits, testimony. Everything you can find, OK?"

Sandi was getting excited. This was for real. "Love it." She reached for a blank sheet of paper, scribbling notes as Len fired off research topics. "I'll just log on and get started."

"Wait, wait. And then you may have to go to the university science library. I want everything you can find on anthrax vaccines and biological agents. A history of who made them, who sold them, and who bought them. Past and present, going back twenty years. Got it?"

As Sandi headed for the door. Len stopped her. "Hold on, finish the copies first. I need them for my meeting this afternoon. Then send out those documents."

"Please." Sandi grabbed Len's sleeve before he could turn away. "Can I take a look at the file?"

"Not yet. Let's see what you come up with and we'll take it from there."

Sandi's heart was pounding and she experienced a sense of pride that she hadn't felt since Joe left. She wanted Len's approval, but so far, he hadn't let her do more than filing, making copies, answering phones, and running errands. This would be the first chance she had to use her brain. She told herself she was just as smart as her brother. She was good at research, good at making connections and she knew it. Maybe, just maybe, she'd be able to use her research skills to pull the facts on Len's client together.

Of course, what she was being asked to do could have been done by a paralegal. If there was one, but there wasn't. Len and Dave ran a bare-bones organization. Not because they couldn't afford more staff. She knew they could. She'd seen their financial records when Lorraine left them on her desk. Len, with all his cases and his drama queen clients, rarely got around to thinking about organizational matters. And Dave was too busy, from what Sandi could tell, worrying about his image to think about ways to improve office functioning.

Sandi finally finished the mountain of photocopies and stacked them in boxes. She took care, printing out labels, and making sure they were properly addressed before she called for the messenger service to pick them up. It was nearly lunchtime when she was ready to log on to the research service.

Two hours later, Sandi was hammering away at the keyboard, squinting at the screen before sending yet another document to the printer. Too bad the office was empty. This was getting interesting, and there was no one she could tell, no one who would understand the implications of what she was reading about Mark Ricklin. She pulled out her cell and dialed Ned.

Her call went to voice mail and she felt like she would burst. She'd just have to wait. She decided to read through what she'd already found, bullet-pointing the information so that Len would be able to get right to the heart of Ricklin's crazy, exotic life. The son of an American engineer father and an English nurse mother, he was born in the Middle East. Along with his siblings, he'd gone to boarding school while his parents took assignments in a variety of inhospitable locations around the globe. He spoke and read several languages, was a computer whiz, and a scientist as well. But despite his rare skills and talents, he never seemed to be able to stick anywhere for long. Always an outsider, drifting from one country to the next, one job to the next, one boss to the next.

Her research was interrupted by the arrival of the messenger to pick up the documents. She pointed to the boxes stacked near the file room. "Have a great night," the young man called to her, maneuvering his hand truck stacked with documents out the door. Only then did Sandi look at the clock and realize it was past five-thirty. Suddenly pangs of hunger overcame her. Her immersion in the task at hand had been complete. Now she realized that except for the candy bar she'd snitched from Lorraine's stash in the drawer, she hadn't eaten since the bagel she'd grabbed at the lobby kiosk over eight hours before. Hunger pangs told her it was time to go. Reluctantly, but with a sense of accomplishment, Sandi printed out a summary and placed it on top of the highlighted articles, slipping everything into her desk drawer.

It was an early spring evening. Even though it wasn't the most direct route home, Sandi decided to cut through the park. Her neck was a little stiff and her back was sore from sitting hours slouched at the keyboard. The walk would do her good, and the breeze carried the promise of better weather ahead. Thank God her next class wasn't until Wednesday. With luck, she could catch up with her work tomorrow. She only hoped that Ned would return her call later tonight. Just in case, she sent a text to remind him.

On the other side of the park, she spotted a platform where a scattering of people stood listening to a man in a camo jacket speaking through a bullhorn. Deciding to avoid the commotion, she was headed toward the exit on the far side of the park when she heard someone call her name. Squinting into the setting sun, she turned toward the voice." Tony is that you?"

Tony broke into a grin. "In the flesh."

"This is your group?" She nodded in the direction of the platform.

"Here, have a brochure." He fanned a stack of leaflets before he stuffed the VETS FOR PEACE literature into his backpack. "Yep, that's us. We're trying to raise awareness before the primary election. One of our members is running for the state legislature, Tom Malory."

"Does he have a chance of getting on the ballot in November?"

"We'll see if a military man with a peace platform can get elected in this state. Should be an interesting campaign. But I'm glad I ran into you."

Sandi laughed. "Run is the operative word. I'm on my way home from the office. And I'd love to chat longer, but I'm starving. When my blood sugar gets low, I get kind of cranky. Haven't eaten since this morning."

"Perfect, let me treat you to dinner. You up for it?"

Sandi nodded.

He turned to his brochure buddy. "Dude, I'm outta here. Catch up later."

Sandi stepped off the curb, oblivious to a car turning the corner. Acting fast, Tony grabbed her arm, pulling her out of the way. "Like I said, when I don't eat, I get a little wobbly." She smiled up at him appreciatively. "Thanks for the save."

"We better get you some food before something serious happens."

Tony took Sandi by the elbow, steering her into the pizza parlor on the corner. "What'll it be plain, or pepperoni? Like I said, when you go with me, you go top drawer."

Once the pizza arrived, Sandi grabbed a slice and tucked in, wasting no time. She devoured a couple more slices in record time before she sat back for a look around. Through the window, she focused on the many pedestrians rushing past. Once again, she realized that, for her, things had changed. She'd become a city dweller, taking comfort in the fact that this was her life; this was home now. Somehow this had helped her to move forward now that Joe was gone.

The intensity of Tony's gaze brought her back to the present and she gave him her full attention. "You never told me where you're from," Sandi said. "We talked about Joe, not much about you."

"I could say the same about you," Tony said.

"My story is not that different from my brother's. We're small-town people. Born in the sticks. Grew up in a factory town. Everybody worked at the plant. Most people grew up, went to school there, got a job there, and so it went. But Joe was never planning to stay in Coatesville, and I guess I've followed in his footsteps."

"My story is kinda the same," said Tony. "Maybe a little different. My folks run a dairy farm in upstate New York, up near the Finger Lakes. Like Joe, I couldn't wait to get out of there. In school, I played a little football, and it got me a scholarship. But after two years of college, I got bored and left. Knocked around for a while, joined the reserves, and then went overseas. Still knocking around, I guess. That's my story. There's not too much more to tell. So, you said you were going to call me?" He took a teasing glance at his watch.

Sandi's face clouded. "Since I saw you, I was planning to get back in touch but I've been so upset about what you told me."

"I understand, and I'm sorry." He took a long sip of soda through a straw.

"Haven't told my folks, but I can't stop thinking about it. Please tell me about Joe…"

"To be honest with you, I wasn't there when he died. We were out on recon."

"But you know." Sandi pulled a tissue from her handbag and wiped her eyes.

"Like I said I wasn't there. But one thing I can tell you is that it wasn't a Humvee accident."

"But why, why? Why did they call it an accident if it wasn't?"

"It's called 'plausible deniability'. If people got word of the way Joe died, there would have been questions to answer and hell to pay."

"All I know is that the casket was sealed. We didn't open it."

"That's what they counted on."

Sandi saw Tony's resolve begin to weaken and so she pressed on. "Please tell me."

Tony's face reflected the inner turmoil. "What I'm about to tell you is classified information, but I'm done with all that. The Army can kiss my ass. The base where we were stationed is called Al Jubayl, in the middle of nowhere, Saudi Arabia. Like Joe, I'd joined the reserves, and we were there to support a U.S. training mission, showing the Saudi military how to use our equipment. To be honest, the Saudi people were not happy about us being there on their soil. The Muslim majority strongly objected to our presence. After everything went down, I found out that our troops were scheduled to leave in a matter of months. Later I heard that one reason the Saudis gave the United States access to their bases was in exchange for the Pentagon turning a blind eye to the Saudi purchase of bioagents."

"Wait, wait. When you say, after everything went down, what do you mean?"

"One night, Joe and I got shit-face drunk and we left our quarters, walking around the base. We got too loud. When the MPs came after us, we ran into a hangar, and Joe opened the wrong door into a restricted area. I don't know what he came in contact with but whatever it was, it made him sick as a dog. A few hours later, we woke up in the brig, but Joe had to go to sickbay. The next day I got sent back to my unit. Nothing more was said to me."

"But what happened to Joe?"

"I kept asking about Joe but nobody spoke up until the captain told me that he was stabilized, that he was gonna be OK. The next day we went out on recon, and when we got back, they told me Joe was gone."

"That was it?"

Nobody was talking. But I heard they brought in a decontamination unit, cleaned up the whole area, and shut down the hangar. Later I heard the MP who went in after Joe and brought him out, he died too."

"So, there was no Humvee accident."

"Like I said, plausible deniability. End of story, no questions asked."

"I should tell my folks."

"Go easy on them. They should know, but if my name gets out, well, like I said, it's classified. I stand to lose big time."

CHAPTER
11

Sandi, perched on the sofa, pulled out her study guide. "You better have your share of the outline for Donovan's class ready on time," she told herself. "If not, they'll kick your ass to the curb, for sure." Just to get her head straight, she Googled the course outline on Tyler's Contract Law: Principles and Cases and began to make a list comparing and contrasting consumer law and business law.

She gulped coffee to stay focused and awake but, too soon, the words on the screen swam in front of her eyes and Tony's voice rang in her ears. His version of Joe's last days reverberated in her head. Plausible deniability. The words brought back flashes of headlines like the story of Jessica Walker, a young soldier the military gave credit for rescuing a whole platoon. More propaganda than fact, that story turned out to be some general's version of a fairytale. Her thoughts turned to the football player who created such a stir when he left the lucrative world of pro sports behind, heading off to fight in Afghanistan instead. How did he die? Friendly fire? It seemed like his family might never know what really happened.

If only Joe had never signed up. Still, when the events of that year came back to her, she remembered why. Dad had been laid off for months. Joe's summer job in construction fell through and he'd ended up slinging burgers. Somebody somewhere told him about tuition the Army offered to undergrads if they signed up for ROTC. It meant he'd be part of the reserves. Back then, before Joe signed up, things were peaceful. Save for minor skirmishes in places nobody ever heard of, there was no expectation that National Guard units would ever be called up.

If only he'd never gone to Saudi Arabia. If only he'd never gotten drunk, never opened that door. He'd still be alive. But what was it? What was behind that door? What could be so lethal that a few seconds of contact with whatever it was spelled death? How could she tell her parents? Even though they weren't gung-ho military, they'd both been so proud of Joe. Could she tell them what Tony told her? Would they call the Pentagon? Demand an investigation? No, she didn't think so. Maybe it was best to let them believe what they'd been told.

Her eyes were dry and scratchy, and her head ached. Sandi didn't know if she'd be able to sleep. She gobbled down a couple of aspirins. In Janine's apartment one floor below, she heard Emily cry out. "Poor kid, she must have had a bad dream."

Sandi dragged herself toward the bedroom wishing she could talk to the one person who would know what to do. But the lump in her throat and the tears stinging her eyes told her that person was dead.

As Len breezed by her desk, Sandi wondered when he'd want to talk about the research he'd asked her to do. She'd already spent a good five hours and then some on her office computer, making sure it was as thorough as possible. That wasn't even counting the trip to the Penn Bio-medical Library to follow up on some of the scholarly journal articles that weren't available online. Sandi was bursting to share what she'd found but Len had his own schedule and his way of doing things. She knew better than to bug him about anything.

She did want to talk, to follow up about hiring a temp at least part-time so she could have time to prepare her assignments and get to class. She hadn't taken this job expecting to work full time and then some, but that's what this was turning out to be.

Where was Dave? She hadn't seen him for the past two days. She checked his online calendar. Saw a cryptic notation and decided to just say he was out of the office and let any clients go to voice mail unless it sounded urgent. But then, none of Dave's clients seemed urgent. She wondered how two guys who worked together could be so different. Maybe that was why things worked. But did they really? The partnership seemed a little lopsided to her, like some marriages. With a shrug, she just put the information in her back pocket for future reference.

Sandi came back from lunch, hoping that there might be some time for her to go over her notes before that night's class on Intellectual Property. She lived in fear that if Donovan called on her, she might stammer a wrong answer the way Ned did the week before. She felt bad about that. Ned wanted to kill her too, and she couldn't blame him. She was responsible for doing the notes on the patents and copyrights section of the reading and when she didn't get it finished, he'd scrambled to fill in for her at the last minute. Was she taking advantage of his more than friendly interest in her? Probably. Sandi always hated the girls in high school that did that and now here she was doing the same thing. She told herself she'd be sure to make it up to him somehow.

She barely noticed the tall skinny guy following her into the elevator. When she pushed six, he smiled at her. Turning back, she stared straight ahead until they got to the sixth floor.

"After you," he gestured.

Sandi got off, frowning to herself. Was this guy following her? He was dressed nice enough, in a tweed jacket, and corduroy trousers. Once again, she found herself, as she often did, trying to retain the details of what people looked like. As if! As if, what? Would she be called to the witness stand to testify? Get a grip!

Thank God Len was in the reception area. "Garrett, good to see you." Len clapped the guy on the shoulder like an old friend. "Say hello to Sandi. She's the new Lorraine."

Garrett's smile widened and Sandi wasn't sure if she should be flattered or insulted. But it felt like the latter and her face burned.

"So, Garrett, what's shakin'?" Len asked.

"What's shakin' today is my nerves. Day Three. No cigarettes."

"Good man. What's your secret?"

"Been to a hypnotist, no luck. Wore the patch, that didn't work. Tried the gum." Garrett pulled a face. "Now I'm going cold turkey. It's rough. Trying to keep busy."

"Perfect timing. Are you up for a little road trip?"

"For you, always."

Len ushered him into the office and closed the door. Sandi checked Len's calendar. The cryptic phrase G. Price Manoaka? stared back at her. *This guy must be G. Price, but what or who was Manoaka?*

She heard laughter coming from behind the door. Taking advantage of the few moments of office quiet she pulled out her notes for tomorrow's class. Commercial Law was so boring. Her head felt heavy and her eyes fought to stay open until Len walked his friend to the door.

Garrett gave Sandi a slice of a grin and a wink on his way past her desk before he turned back to Len. "I'll be sure to send you a postcard from End of Forever, West Virginia. What's the name of that town again?"

"Listen carefully. It's M-A-N-O-A-K-A. Now repeat after me, Man-oak-a."

Garrett cracked up. "Got it! Manoaka."

Sandi went back and forth. *Wait until he asks you.* Impulse control was never her strong suit. *Don't make a fool of yourself by offering your grade school interpretations of what you found.* A teacher in junior high, Mrs. Vance, once told her to count to ten and then count again before she shouted out answers in class. Did the teacher say the same thing to the boys? No, Sandi didn't think so. It made her blood boil to always be told to sit down, be quiet, and wait to be called on. That was for wimps.

Len was always on the phone, having intense, but sincere counseling sessions with his clients, their spouses, or a reporter from one newspaper or another. Even though he'd lost the case, he'd made a reputation for himself in a sensational murder trial where the client was convicted of killing his family. When she read the book about it, she'd thought the client was guilty, but now she wasn't so sure. In jail now for seven or eight years, the man still claimed his innocence. Lorraine had told her that Len stayed in touch with what was going on. A couple of private detectives were still on the case, still trying to track the alleged perpetrators the husband claimed had committed the murders. When she'd asked Lorraine where things stood. Her office mate answered, "Len calls it a stone-cold case."

Looking down at the telephone console, she saw Len's line was free. For now, he wasn't on the phone. Unable to stop herself, she lingered outside in his doorway. "Knock, knock. Have a minute?"

Looking up, Len signaled agreement but Sandi knew she had to talk fast. "I've been thinking about Mark's case. I read his deposition and I think he's telling the truth."

Len swiveled back in his brown leather chair. "Let's hear it. Talk to me."

Feeling encouraged, Sandi plowed ahead. She took a breath. "Something happened. I just found out. Joe didn't die the way they said."

"OK?" Len's eyebrows knit together in a squiggly line. His forehead wrinkled. "But Mark? What does that have to do…?"

"Mark's company, Vectelon, makes biological materials that are lethal."

"That's the story."

"When he was overseas, Joe accidentally came in contact with some kind of germs that killed him."

"What about the accident? Wasn't there some kind of Humvee explosion?"

"That was the version the Pentagon told us. Since then, I found out different. They didn't want to admit anything, you know."

Down the corridor, a man in black pants and a jacket with purple trim appeared. "Fed Ex? Can somebody sign?"

Len nodded his head toward the hallway, and Sandi took the cue for her to go handle the delivery. Trying to hold the moment, she turned back. "What I'm asking is, please can you let me help on this case? Let me do more?"

"I'll think about it." His cell phone began to vibrate. Squinting at the screen, he took the call.

CHAPTER
12

Sometimes, people asked Garrett if he'd ever been a cop. When that happened, he usually muttered a few words and tried to change the subject. Sure, he'd been a cop. Hadn't they all? He'd like to know one private investigator who hadn't started out that way. He was a cop for six years. Only just long enough to break up his marriage to Deirdre. Of course, with his wife calling him a bad influence, he'd had a hard time in court getting visitation to see his kids. Luckily the judge didn't agree with his wife's opinion.

After the divorce, he'd lost his ability to concentrate. Even his street smarts seemed to disappear. After being shot in the middle of a drug raid, he'd gone out on disability. Those were the two years he'd spent home alone drinking and smoking, watching true crime TV, and working his way to the grave. Thank God that psychologist helped him find his way back. She'd gotten him into rehab. The staff there told him he had an addictive personality. He didn't agree but he stopped drinking anyway. Now, it was just the cigarettes. If he found himself standing behind a smoker on the street, he caught himself inhaling deeply.

He couldn't help himself. People said he'd grow to hate the smell of cigarette smoke, but he couldn't imagine when that would be.

Just for the feel of it, he pulled the plastic cigarette from his desk drawer and placed it between his lips. Tapping the computer keyboard, he squinted at the screen and jotted a few words on a scrap of paper. Looking for his phone, Garrett patted down the piles of documents and yellowing file folders stacked in ragged piles on the flat surfaces of his desk, the filing cabinet, and the old typewriter table that circled the periphery of his place of business. Locating the missing item under a fast-food wrapper, he put his feet up, leaned back, and dialed.

"Hey there." Garrett smiled to add warmth to his voice. "Is this the Manoaka Chronicle?" On the other end of the phone, he imagined the hillbilly version of the one-horse town. Still, the voice that came back sounded young, sharp, and intelligent with nary a twang. After a few warm-up questions, Garrett asked, "Have you heard of any weird infections or maladies out your way?"

"Yeah, there was something like that some months back, right before I got here. Two men from the reservation, tribe members had died. It didn't sound like foul play. You know there'd been that scare about the hantavirus or swine flu or bird flu, something like that. Not sure what it was. I can't check it right now, but if you want to give me a call back tomorrow, I'll see what I can find."

CHAPTER
13

Going north on I-95, Greta had felt anonymous, but now, here in the middle of nowhere, she felt vulnerable, visible. Too visible. She looked into the rearview. A panel truck whizzed by, too fast for her to catch the logo, then darkness was behind her. She pulled off onto the shoulder and squinted at her GPS. She'd programmed the intersection that Len gave her, just over the Delaware state line like he'd said. According to the annoying voice of her GPS, she'd already made a few wrong turns. But she seemed to be going the right way now. She disabled the voice, deciding that, worst-case scenario; she could give Len a call if she didn't find him in the next five minutes.

Greta moved past the little strip mall and took a right next to the railroad tracks. Up ahead, a pair of headlights flashed, and she knew they were for her. She pulled in next to Len's car. They hadn't met before but she'd seen him speak at a panel a few years ago and remembered what he looked like.

Len's smile was reassuring. Their driver's side windows paralleled each other and if she'd wanted to, she could have just passed the papers across to him through the open windows. Not that she'd do that, but the thought did occur. Len squeezed out of his car and came around to her passenger side. Greta unlocked the door, and Len slid in next to her. "How was the drive up from D.C.? Traffic, OK?"

Greta nodded. They made small talk, playing the "Who do you know in D.C." game for a few minutes, getting more comfortable with each other. When Len asked Greta if she had any kids, she shook her head, "No."

"Well, maybe that's for the best. My kid told me a lawyer joke last night. Want to hear it?" He asked without waiting for her to agree. "Did you hear about the new microwave lawyer? You spend eight minutes in his office, and you get billed as if you'd been there for eight hours."

Greta laughed, grateful for a break in the tension. Still, she wanted to tell him that she didn't think anyone had followed her. In reality, she didn't want to even acknowledge that was a possibility, although, sadly, she knew it was.

"I always considered myself the loyal employee type, so this is kinda hard for me."

"Understood, so what have you got for me?"

As Greta pulled a briefing paper from within her briefcase, Len flicked on a mini flashlight and spent several minutes poring over the paperwork.

"Tribal lands? Pretty slick." He sat back and turned off the light. "The reservation is a sovereign entity. So, the contract between Vectelon and the tribe? It's off the books. Federal laws don't apply."

"That was the general idea. It's been going on longer than you would believe. It started when they were producing vaccines. Then they shut down the contract and that's when they switched to working on the actual viruses. Now with the possibility of casino income, the tribe wants the company off their land."

"Not surprised. Got anything else?"

"That's it for now. Let's see where this takes us. I'm doing this for Mark." Greta said. "I know he's crazy, but still, I feel responsible."

"You? Why?"

"Didn't he tell you? I helped him get the job at Vectelon; I gave him a reference. Because of that, I'm already under a lot of scrutiny. They're looking for a scapegoat. If my boss finds out I gave anything to Mark's lawyer, I'm dead. My career is over."

"Don't worry. We'll make sure nobody knows where this came from."

Ken Daley's serge-clad buttocks rested on the edge of his desk. If he'd looked out the window, five floors down, he'd have seen Washington's evening traffic as it crawled away from Capitol Hill toward the suburbs. Instead, he studied the photos spread across the glass-topped mahogany surface. After a moment of silence, he looked up at the two men in front of him. Both in suits and ties, their close-cropped hair and bearing suggested military training. The men leaned closer.

"Based on your photos, looks like you've come up with some interesting connections." Ken picked up a shot of Greta and Len taken with a night vision scope next to a bridge. He flicked the edge of the photo with the tips of his fingers. He shook his head knowingly. "Do you believe it? I should have known. Loyalty's a thing of the past."

One by one, Ken selected photos of Dave and Len, standing outside on a Philadelphia street. There was another shot of Sandi and Len in front of the parking garage. He gazed at them for several minutes. Daly slid the photos into a file folder, pushing it across to the younger man. "Be sure to send me copies of all of these shots."

"These are for you. Keep them. We have duplicates." He pointed to an aluminum briefcase next to the desk. The older of the two nodded in agreement. "Ken, let us do our job. We're here to solve your problems."

"That's what I want to hear. Gentlemen, I'm putting this in your hands."

Daly walked the two men to the door. "From now on, just call me on the number I gave you." He slapped the older guy on the back. "Stop me if you've heard this one. A lawyer is having a meeting with the devil. So, Satan says…"

As the men exited laughing, Ken watched them walk to the elevator and push the down button. He turned back with a smirk.

CHAPTER
14

Sandi walked up and down the aisles that divided the study carrels in the law library. Her first year of law school, this had been her second home. Feeling a twinge of guilt, she couldn't help thinking that she should be spending more time here. As it was, she'd only been here once or twice this semester, and even then, it was just to pick up a book on reserve. Checking out her old haunt, she caught a glimpse of Ned's reddish-brown curls lolling to the side, glasses askew, head resting on his hand. She leaned toward his ear and whispered, "Counselor, the judge wants to see you in his chambers."

Ned startled awake. He jerked his head around, rubbing his eyes. Spying Sandi sitting next to him, he gave her arm a playful punch. "Hey, Sandi. Very funny."

"I tracked you down."

"So, I see. You ready to go over the outline?"

"Ned, wait. First, let's talk. I need your help."

"Why am I not surprised?

Sandi dragged an empty chair across the floor, and sat, leaning in. "It's not that," she said. "My outline can wait."

"Then, what?"

"I need you to go to West Virginia with me."

"What are you talking about?" Ned's voice notched up a level or two. "You totally lost me."

The next aisle over, students rustled papers and hissed for quiet. Sandi stood, dragging Ned from his chair. She beckoned him toward the red exit sign.

Eyebrows knit into a frown; Ned followed her into the beige cinderblock stairwell. They perched on the window ledge, ignoring the late afternoon sun throwing a pale light on Temple University's teeming urban campus.

Ned looked Sandi squarely in the eye. "Now, what are you talking about?"

Sandi peered from side to side as if other ears were nearby. "At the firm, we have that client…you know, the scientist I told you about?"

"Yeah, Dr. Deadly?"

"Very funny. Anyway, there's something weird going on and I need to find out what they do there."

"What who does where? I thought he was in jail."

"He is. I'm talking about the company he worked for, Vectelon. They have some kind of strange lab in West Virginia! I need to see it firsthand. Will you go with me?"

Ned shrugged, his expression trying for bored acquiescence. "OK, I'll do it."

But to Sandi, somehow, his expression came across as *I'll do anything for you.* She smiled, ruffling his curls. "Great, pick you up tomorrow at seven a.m."

"But that's the week-end."

"You have plans?"

"Yeah, but no, but. OK, I'll go."

"Cool, see you then."

CHAPTER
15

Sandi didn't think too hard about whether she'd pushed Ned further than she should have. Although they were the same age, he often complained that she treated him like her mascot or maybe her kid brother. More than once, he'd told her, "You don't take me seriously."

So far, he'd been willing to do most things she asked of him. He seemed happy enough to take over the driving after they stopped for brunch or whatever you wanted to call a fast-food egg and soggy muffin combo at the Breezewood rest stop on the Pennsylvania Turnpike. Still, she felt a little guilty after he complained, saying," The least you could do was to stay awake long enough to tell me where to turn after we left Pennsylvania."

"Ned. I'm sorry I was starting to feel a little car sick after we ate. I took a couple of Dramamine. I forgot that sometimes it makes me drowsy. "

They were in Maryland now. "It should just be another hour or so," she lied. According to her calculations, it was another hour to the West Virginia state line. Then they would have another two and a half hours to reach the southwestern part of the state that was their destination.

As the miles flew by, Sandi remembered other road trips that were part of her family's vacation lore. The time they drove to Disneyworld in Florida after Dad won the five nights at the Disney hotel for being "employee of the year". They could have flown but Mom said the thought of flying made her nervous. On the way down, Sandi remembered being car sick in the backseat, and they had to stop a few times to take care of what ailed her.

Today's drive took a lot longer than she'd expected and shadows had begun to lengthen by the time Sandi spied the sign welcoming them to Manoaka. The poor mountain hamlet ran just four blocks on either side of the town's main drag. Sandi counted off two churches, a gas station, beauty parlor, and general store. A sign advertised regular meetings of the Manoaka Rotary Club on the first Thursday of every month at the Elk Hall.

"Looks like we just missed it." Sandi giggled, pointing to the meeting's notice.

"Shucks," Ned drawled.

Sandi was relieved that Ned didn't seem to have lost his sense of humor. If their roles were reversed, she'd want to kill him by now.

"Now are you finally going to tell me what it is that we're looking for in this God-forsaken town?" Ned asked. "It had better be juicy enough to make this trip worthwhile."

"You'll see. Keep going. I'll know it when we get there." Would she know it? Sandi wasn't sure. She squinted at the map that showed a featureless trapezoidal shape blocked out in pale green that was labeled Manoaka Reservation. As the Manoaka town center disappeared in the rearview mirror, Ned turned on the headlights to counter the darkness on the curving two-lane road spooling out ahead of them through the pines.

"Slow down. We must be getting close." Around the bend, a gated entrance on the right warned **No Trespassing-Private Tribal Lands**. Noting the guard stationed near a gate at the bottom of a grassy incline, Sandi hissed, "Don't stop. Just keep on going."

"Well, that was fun," Ned sneered.

After what felt like another mile, Ned found a spot on the shoulder and made a U-turn. "Ready to go home?"

"Very funny," Sandi punched his shoulder. She pointed to a cut-off sign that read, *Truck Weigh-in Station - Closed*. "I don't think anyone will bother us there. Pull in."

"Do you have to be so bossy?" Still, Ned did as he was told and the two settled down to wait for nightfall. Sandi pulled her jacket closer around her shoulders and closed her eyes but Ned was having none of that.

"Wanna go over our notes?"

At Sandi's look, he laughed. "Just kidding. Hand me one of those sandwiches?"

Sandi retrieved her backpack from the back seat and pulled out some food. "We should wait until it's pitch dark. Wake me in an hour if I fall asleep."

Long after darkness had fallen, Sandi and Ned still slept soundly. Ned's eyes fluttered open and he cracked the door to the car, got out, and stood outside to relieve himself. Climbing back into the driver's seat, he shook Sandi awake.

"What time is it?" she asked.

"It's almost midnight."

"OMG, how did that happen?" Sandi checked her watch.

"Let me think," said Ned with a mocking tone to his voice, "We got up at the crack of dawn, drove to the middle of nowhere, and fell asleep in the woods."

Driving back the way they came in, they noticed that there was only one man inside the guard station. They drove further. "Keep on going, keep going," Sandi said. "I want to see what's on the other side of the fence. "

Further on, they hid the car in a wooded incline on the other side of the road. Sliding out of the old Volvo, Sandi pretended not to notice Ned's raised eyebrows, the whistling under his breath, the looks he gave her that seemed to be questioning her sanity. Sandi looked over her shoulder, checking to make sure Ned was still with her as she searched for a spot along the chain link fence where she could climb over.

Ned hung back. "Have you considered the fact that we might get shot?"

"I think it's dark enough now that we can't be seen. I'm going ahead." But Ned's thought struck home. "If you want, you can go back to the car. I won't blame you." In seconds, Sandi was up and over the fence.

Following her lead, Ned heaved over, slipping to the other side. Sandi lent a hand, relieved to see him get up and brush the dirt off the knees of his jeans.

"You OK?"

"No, are you? What if we fell?" Ned said. "I should have brought the flashlight?"

Sandi pointed to a flicker of firelight cutting through the darkness. Silently, she nudged her reluctant companion forward.

Moving closer, they saw a domed structure covered in a rough patchwork of canvas. Nearby a column of flames shot sparks up into the night sky. Drums throbbed from within. Faint sounds of chanting grew in the night air. Protected by the trees, Ned stayed out of the clearing, but Sandi snuck closer, leaning in as the swell of voices grew.

"Great spirit, hear our voices. Send this evil from our land. We call on you to cleanse our tribe.

Purify us." The drumming built to a peak. Then there was silence. The flap was thrown back and steam poured forth, condensing in the chilly night air.

Ned motioned Sandi back out of the light. Moving away from the flames and the sound of the drums, the pair were soon scrambling around trees and over rocks. Once they made the high ground, they looked down wide-eyed at a strange sight spread before them in the valley below.

In a scene as bright as day, two one-story buildings, illuminated from within by fluorescent lighting, stood surrounded by a high chain link fence. A guard kept watch at the door of the larger building. Beyond the second building, two big rigs and a fleet of smaller white vans were parked in orderly rows. Sandi and Ned silently took in what they saw. "This is so weird," Sandi whispered. "Something tells me these people with the trucks surely are not members of the tribe."

Inching down the incline, Sandi jumped, stifling a screech as a critter skittered across her path. Creeping as close as they dared, she and Ned hid behind the last few bushes, providing cover. Dismayed at the fence and the lights, Ned grabbed Sandi's sleeve. "C'mon, let's get out of here. This is too weird."

As they watched, an 18-wheeler roared to life. The electronic gate slid open, allowing the big rig to exit the compound. As the truck faded away down the road, the lights on the gate flickered out. Sandi grabbed Ned and pulled him to his feet. "Now!"

Just before it clanged shut, they managed to slip through the electronic gate. Slithering between two parked vans, Sandi pointed to the exterior rear door of the smaller building, closest to where they now hid in the parking lot. Fluorescent light from within the structure shone through a window. Before Ned could react, Sandi darted out, slipping around the corner of the building. Crouching by the window, she peeked in and her mouth dropped open. "Oh my God, it is a laboratory," she whispered to herself. "Out here in the middle of nowhere."

Inside two men, encased in hazmat gear, breathing apparatus attached, moved around the glass-enclosed interior, packing dozens of sealed metal thermos-type receptacles into crates. Cages of animals lined the walls. A sign on the wall read **Vectelon Corporation**.

Sandi motioned for Ned, who hung back. His face signaled fear before his head ducked out of sight. As he crouched near a van, two guards shouted back and forth.

"Going to Millie's for coffee. Whaddya want?"

"I'll have it black, and bring me back an egg sandwich."

Sandi jumped as a stone hit her foot. She looked in Ned's direction. His head motioned toward the guard moving their way. Sandi watched Ned as he looked frantically for a hiding place. Then he slipped behind the van, tried the door, and slid inside.

Sandi held her breath as the guard unlocked the van closest to the gate, settled himself inside, and turned the key. With the guard now inside the van, she ran to where she had last seen Ned. When she opened that van door and slid inside to hide with him, Ned's eyes bulged with a mixture of fear and anger.

"Are you crazy?" he whispered.

Sandi felt like Ned wanted to kill her.

"Once this guard leaves, I'm out of here," Ned said. "If you're smart, you will be too."

A few feet away, an engine sputtered and revved, but failed to start. The driver's curses filled the air. "Goddam day shift. Fill up the fucking tank, why don't you?" He got out, slamming the door of the nonfunctioning van behind him.

As the sound of footsteps on gravel moved closer, Ned and Sandi each held their breath, flattening themselves out on the floor of the van. Muttering to himself, the guard fumbled with the key ring until, finding what he needed, he stuck the key in the lock and opened the door. Heaving his weight behind the wheel, he started the engine and shifted gears, ready to pull out, his two frightened passengers hiding in the rear.

Ahead of the van, a second tractor-trailer, lights on, waited for the gate to open. Aside from the hazmat symbols on the sides, the trailer itself was blank. Only the door of the white cab, with its intertwined initials VI, identified it as Vectelon Industries. The security guard waved the big rig through.

From inside the cab, the driver waved. "That's it. One more load and we'll be out of here."

"Shuttin' it down temporary?"

"No. Don't you know? What I heard, they're gassin' the animals and calling it quits."

"Goddam, this time next week, we'll be filing for unemployment."

The driver laughed, "Could be. Wouldn't be the first time."

The big rig lumbered out to the road, its fumes tainting the pine-scented air of the mountains. Behind the rig, the van driver turned in the opposite direction, hit the gas, and peeled out. "Finally," he said. "A guy could starve to death around here."

Only after the van turned onto the stretch of road that headed back to town, did Sandi and Ned dare to lift their heads from the floor. As they exchanged looks of dismay, the driver turned on the radio, and the van filled with the sounds of hillbilly rap.

Moving south on I-95, Garrett felt his shoulders relax as the sounds of Mahler filled the interior of his Jeep. He still loved Mahler's 9th; it always had a way of soothing his nerves. Some called it a little sad, but he'd loved it since junior high when he played in the school orchestra. The only reason he'd even gone along with playing an instrument was so he could spend time ogling the music teacher, Ms. Zimmerman. Looking back now, he realized she wasn't the beauty his seventh-grade eyes took her to be. But she always carried herself as if she were. Trailing perfume and fluttery silk scarves, she was the closest he'd ever gotten to glamour in the rural school district in upstate Pennsylvania where he lived. So, there was that.

He loved hearing the stories about the lives of the composers that she read to them during music class. Stories of intrigue and drama set in Vienna, Rome, or Florence. All those places he'd barely heard about came to life as the artists starved in attics, all while currying favor, fighting off their rivals, and petitioning nobles for commissions. He loved the drama of it and thought maybe if he'd lived in that time, he might have done well in one of those royal courts.

Yes, Garret could imagine himself in the royal courts of Europe. He wouldn't have been a courtier himself, no, probably not. But perhaps he would have been one of those trusted underlings who carried out the directions and lurked behind doors, listening to the plots and conspiracies that swirled around the rich and powerful. Outwitting those with plans to overthrow the reigning aristocracy, he liked to think he would have used his superior gamesmanship. But was it gamesmanship really or a "second sight," as his mother said? Whatever it was, at an early age, he found that he could see several steps ahead of the game whether it was, Parcheesi, checkers, or later, chess.

As the second movement ended, Garrett felt himself patting his pockets for a cigarette and then he remembered. "Shit." He wondered if he should pull off at the Delaware line, get some gum or mints to keep himself going. He was headed to the woods of Appalachia. God knows what he might or might not come across there.

Eyes straying to the rearview, he frowned at the sight of the silverish sedan two cars back. Something about the guy driving had caught his attention before. And now, here he was again. Garrett pulled off at the exit ramp. He found a

Seven-Eleven and stocked up on something to distract his taste buds. He figured if the tail was serious, he'd show up again and then Garrett would know for sure.

To curb his agitation, he started the Mahler over again. They were on the third movement when he spotted that car behind him again. In a maneuver, Garrett slammed off the highway exit, careening down an embankment before he turned right onto a local road. A hundred feet ahead, he spied a gravel drive next to a stand of trees. Taking the driveway, he pulled between the trees, cutting the lights and the motor.

In his wake, horns blared as the silver sedan slammed into reverse, backing into oncoming traffic to get back to the exit ramp. If it weren't so late at night, Garrett swore that the car would have been dust. Making the exit ramp, the car tracked Garrett's route but missed the gravel path. From behind the stand of pines, Garrett grinned as they continued down the road. "That's it, you bastards. Keep going."

From underneath the seat, Garrett extracted a metal box. Pulling the keys from the ignition, they unlocked the box. Inside was a fresh pack of menthols. Tapping the pack, he opened it, pulled out a cig, lit it, and exhaled deeply, allowing himself a few more drags before he threw the smoke out the window and returned to the highway. Back on I-95, he found himself passing the first exit over the Maryland line. Then he headed northwest on 273. Instinct told him to take the local roads, and he pulled into the next gas station to check his route.

In the rear of the van, Sandi and Ned hugged the floor and each other in an attempt to keep from bouncing, jostling, and making any noise. Sandi bit her tongue when she felt a hole open up in the knee of her jeans after she'd scraped a bolt on the van's floor. Thank God, the driver blasted what sounded like Kenny McChesney from his speakers. Sandi hoped the music was loud enough that he would be deaf to any sounds they might make in their desperate effort to stay hidden. What could happen if, in the worst-case scenario, their presence was discovered? As long as the guard wasn't carrying a gun, she guessed they would survive with little exterior damage.

She knew she owed Ned big time for this one and wondered how she could ever repay him for his help. Her thoughts were stilled as the van made a hard left and they bounced against the side of the van and each other. With a final hit of the breaks, Sandi heard a crunch as Ned's head banged into her elbow. Ned groaned and then was silent. The driver turned off the music, exiting the van with a slam of the door.

Sandi, on her back now, rolled her head over softly. She was sickened to see Ned's eyes closed and a scrape of blood on his forehead. "Ned, Ned. I'm so sorry. Oh my God, Ned! Are you OK?"

Slowly, Ned's eyes opened. "Oh, my head. It feels like my eyes don't want to focus. Where are we?"

Sandi looked out the rear van window, glad to see the guard had entered the café, and taken a seat at the counter, his back to the door. Overhead the neon sign read, "Millie's 24/7 Café. We never close." She lifted herself into a crouch and tried to help Ned scoot himself toward the door. Ned made a quick exit, but Sandi's eyes fell on a manila folder stuck inside a basket of nylon webbing on the back of the driver's side.

Ned looked back, "Sandi," he hissed. "C'mon. Now!"

Reaching around, she grabbed the folder. Papers in hand, she closed the van's rear door, and together they ran, with Ned hobbling across the lot toward the pine forest surrounding the café, the parking lot, and just about everything else in the state of West Virginia. Safe within the trees they looked at each other with relief. Sandi broke into hysterical laughter and planted a huge kiss on Ned. Despite his pain, he beamed and pulled her into his arms, kissing her with a passion that caught Sandi off guard.

Sandi waited for the moment to pass. "Let's think of what our next step should be?"

Ned looked incredulous. "What our next step should be is to get the fuck out of here. How far do you think we are from the car?"

"Let's wait until the driver leaves the diner. Then, we'll walk back that way. It's probably going to be at least three or four miles. I wonder if we should try to hitch a ride?"

"Well, it's for sure, there's no taxi service around here."

Sandi felt a little better after hearing Ned crack a joke. "How's your head?"

After searching his head for bumps, Ned touched his battered eye with care. "I guess I'll live."

Sandi held up the folder, waving the documents like a trophy. "At least we have something to show for the injury."

"You have something to show. I've got the headache."

"I'm sorry. I don't mean to be so oblivious." She reached over, briefly placing a hand on Ned's shoulder. "I wasn't even thinking about any danger. I was thinking of Joe. I did it for Joe."

"I don't get it, but if Joe was watching, I'm sure he'd have wanted to kick your ass."

"No, he wouldn't." She gave Ned a playful punch on the arm. "Let's get something to eat. I'm starved."

As soon as the van driver finished his coffee, picked up his order, and drove off, they headed inside. The waitress behind the counter welcomed the pair. "Help yourselves. Sit anywhere."

No longer needing to hide, they took a table by the window and looked out into the dark. Soon their attention turned to the menu. Within minutes, Ned nodded to the waitress, letting her know that they were ready. Eagerly, they both ordered eggs, home fries, and coffee.

"Oh, and I'll have the bacon. We can share." Sandi nudged Ned. "Says it's the Bennett County Fair prize-winning bacon."

A black Jeep drove into the lot, pulled around the side, and cut its lights. As a man with a baseball hat pulled low got out and walked into the café, Sandi's jaw dropped. "Oh, my God! This is amazing. That's Garrett."

"Who?"

Sandi hissed. "The private investigator. I told you about him."

Garrett took a seat in a corner away from the window and removed his cap.

Sandi got up. "Wait right here."

Ned's mouth dropped open as he watched her approach the baseball cap man. The man's thin-lipped countenance didn't loosen at the sight of Sandi even as she slid into a seat across from him.

"You're Garrett, right? Don't you remember? It's me, Sandi from Krause and Nielsen?"

"What the hell are you doing here?"

"Len asked me to come and take some pictures of the town."

Garrett's eyes seemed to roll back in his head at this news. He reached for his phone and dialed. His brows came together as he squinted at the "No Service" message on the screen.

The waitress arrived with the coffee pot. Turning his cup over, Garrett nodded in her direction. The waitress eyed Sandi. "You want me to bring your eggs over here?"

Sandi motioned to Ned to join the party. He slid in next to her and several seconds later, their platters were served. As they dug in, Garrett's eyes closed for a few seconds.

"Rough drive?" Ned asked.

"Yeah, you could say that." Garrett eyed Ned's swollen eye. "Looks like I'm not the only one having a rough time. What happened to you?"

Sandi nudged Ned in the ribs. "He slipped on some gravel and fell."

"So, what kind of photographs? Where's your camera."

Sandi shrugged. "Left it in the car. Can you give us a lift back down the road?"

"I got an early appointment. I'll drop you off after. Where are you parked?"

"On the other side of town, past the reservation."

Garrett took it in, nodding agreement. Sipping his coffee, he continued to try for service on his phone. "Must be the mountains, I'm getting nothing."

Sandi and Ned finished their food and Ned signaled the waitress for the bill.

Garrett squinted at his watch. "Getting late. I'm planning to grab a few hours of shut-eye, gonna sleep in the car. If you want, you're welcome to sleep in the back seat.

On the way out, Garrett ordered a large coffee to go and paid for all of them. "I'll make my stop after daybreak. You two wait in the car, OK?"

Sandi nodded agreement as Ned yawned.

At sunrise, Garrett pulled past the Manoaka Church of God on the right. "Looks like we're too early for church," he muttered, chuckling at his own humor. The main drag was Sunday morning empty except for a pick-up outside the storefront office of the Bennett County Courier. Garrett parked next to it. He turned to Sandi, "You two wait here."

Garrett tried the door for the storefront. When it opened. He called out, "Jesse?"

A young man looked up from his computer. "You Garrett?" He squinted through the frameless glasses that fell over his nose. "Looks like you found us OK." He peered past the investigator's shoulder, his glance skimming over the occupants outside in the car.

Garrett followed his glance. "Brought a couple of interns along with me."

"Hit a lot of traffic?"

Garret decided not to think about the car that had followed him. "Not much after I got out of Pennsylvania. But anyway, real nice little town you got here."

"Thanks. I heard it was real quiet too. Until they came."

"Who's they?"

"Vectelon. This might be what you are looking for. Here's an article from a few years ago, back when they first showed up."

The young journalist read the headline aloud. "Defense contractor signs contract with Manoaka elders - promises jobs for tribe."

Garrett took the folder, thumbing through it.

"Only just now getting our backfile of articles scanned."

"Call me old school. I got no problem with paper files." Garrett sat quiet, reading the articles.

"Vectelon, they managed to fly under the radar for a while," Jesse said. "Made the tribe promise not to use their name."

He looked up at the reporter. "So, what changed things?"

"A while back, the county health service tried to quarantine the res. There was concern about what they were testing in there."

"And…?"

"Tribe claimed the state had no jurisdiction, but the health service disagreed. If I was you, I'd be talking to the doctor there."

Sandi showed up suddenly at Garrett's elbow. Peering over his shoulder, she tried for a glimpse of the folder's contents, but he blocked her view.

"I told you to wait in the car, didn't I?" Garrett turned from Sandi back to the puzzled reporter. "Sorry. Where'd you say that office was?"

"Didn't. It's over in Tuckerville. You come in on 93, right? Maybe twenty minutes further south."

Garrett stood, "I'll find it," he said as he handed the reporter an envelope. The young man looked up mystified. "Little something for your trouble," Garrett said, closing the door.

On the other side of town, near the reservation, Sandi and Ned hopped out of the car. "Garrett. Thanks again. You saved our lives."

Making a U-turn, he gave them a farewell wave. "See ya back in Philly." His smile was ironic.

"O-my-God! What a night! You OK to drive?" Ned asked.

Feeling strangely keyed up, Sandi turned the key in the ignition. "Yeah, I'm good."

Ned looked surprised. "You sure?"

They headed back into town, stopping in front of the news office. Without a word, Sandi got out, heading inside. For the second time, the reporter looked up with a surprised expression.

"Hi, Garrett told us to follow him, but we got separated. Can you show me where he went?" She stuck a map under the young guy's nose.

The reporter traced a route. "Should have stayed on 93 like I told him."

"He did, but we got stuck behind a logging truck, and he went on ahead. What was the name of the person you told him to call?"

"Didn't give him a name but if I was going to talk to anybody, who it'd probably be?" Here he looked back at an article on the computer screen. "It would be Haynes, Dr. Elizabeth Haynes."

Sandi waved her thanks and smiled a farewell.

Back in the car, Sandi looked at the map. "He went south. Someplace called Tuckerville. Shove over. We're looking for someone, a doctor named Haynes."

Ned obliged, squinting at the folded map Sandi dropped on the seat. He sighed, "OK, off to Tuckerville. But FYI, I wasn't banking on a week-long expedition. My folks were supposed to come into town tonight. Meet me for dinner."

"Sorry to put you through all this. Probably a Greyhound bus stop somewhere."

"You gotta be kidding me. Where do you think we are? If there is a bus that goes through here, it's maybe once a day, and who knows where it stops."

"Seriously. Do you want me to take you back to Manoaka? That reporter was pretty nice. He might know more."

"Yeah, right. Sure, just drive me back. Like that's what you'd do. Keep going. I'll call my folks and tell them to catch me next week-end instead."

Sandi considered Ned's sarcasm, then shrugged. "There's the sign for Route 93." They made the turn-off and continued south in silence.

Sandi's Volvo slowed, cruising past a white fence post separating the manicured lawn from the road. The rural mailbox read E. Haynes.

"You think this is it?" Ned asked.

"How many Haynes could there be? You coming?"

Ned shook his head.

Sandi headed up the path to a Civil War-era frame house, front porch bedecked with two faded birch rockers, both having seen better days. Before she could knock a fortyish lab-coated woman opened the door. On her way out, she startled, faltering on the threshold.

"Ooh. Sorry, didn't expect company. Help you?" In one motion, the woman pushed glasses up on her nose and tossed dark hair out of her eyes.

"Didn't mean to scare you. You're Dr. Haynes?"

Head cocked to the side she gave Sandi a quizzical once over. Then she pulled the front door closed, testing it to make sure it locked. "Yes, can I help you?"

"A reporter at the Manoaka Courier gave me your name."

"OK, sorry to rush you but I'm late," Haynes said. "You seem to know who I am. And you are?"

"Didn't mean to be so rude. Sandi Brennan." She stuck out her hand.

The doctor gave it the briefest of shakes and moved down the steps toward her driveway. "On call. Got to go."

"Please, just a second. We've driven all the way from Philadelphia."

Haynes turned on the gravel path. "Why?"

"Our firm has a client who… It's about what happened at the reservation."

"You mean the two men?"

Sandi had no idea what she was talking about but hid her confusion. "Well, yes. Of course, and what is going on out there."

"I'm gonna talk fast. If you want to take notes."

Sandi pulled a small tablet from her bag and dug for a pen.

"It started with Jonas Roundtree. He came into the health service with what looked like the flu. I took a culture and gave him an antibiotic that should have knocked it out. But by the end of the week, Jonas was dead. His friend Grant died two days later."

"What was it?"

"Couldn't be sure. I sent the cultures to the state lab for testing. They came back inconclusive but after Jonas died, we wanted to inoculate everyone on the reservation."

"Where did it come from?"

"From the animals. From the test subjects in the lab."

"I've seen it," Sandi remembered the van driver's question to the guard and his response about killing the lab animals.

"You've seen it? Nobody in town even knew what was there until Jonas got sick. Of course, they saw the trucks coming and going. But it was all on the down low."

Sandi thought back to their late-night ride in the van and wondered what she and Ned might have been exposed to. She knew she'd have to tell Ned, and then what?

"The reservation's council of elders has always been pretty forthcoming, but not this time. God knows what they were exposed to."

Sandi paused in her note-taking. A question died on her lips as ringtones from the doctor's cell gave them both a start.

"I'm sorry." Haynes unlocked her car and slid behind the wheel. "I've got to go."

CHAPTER
16

For the first time, Sandi was scared. Now that she was standing in front of Len in his office, the impact of what they'd done, the craziness of it, hit her.

Len's face, usually framed by eyebrows raised in amusement or curiosity now expressed his anger. "You did what?"

"Then we jumped out of the van and ran into the woods."

"I can't believe this. I have someone who is certifiable on the payroll. What were you thinking?"

"Len, wait. I know you're mad. But just take a look. The most important thing is this. Please." Sandi held out the document she'd taken from the van.

Len grabbed it and read aloud from the bold print. "Shipping Confirmation, Vectelon Biotechnology Division. Anthrax culture – 1000 units."

"If I had to make a judgment call, I'd say they were clearing the place out, shipping everything out of there. I heard the driver tell the guard they were shutting it down."

Sandi's fear changed to exultation as she saw the look of surprise beginning to spread over his face. "Do you know what this is?"

"Proof? Is this the proof you've been looking for?"

Relief flooded Sandi's heart. She watched Len's face slowly relax into his more usual countenance. He came around the desk to give her a hug. "Kid, you are gonna make one hell of a lawyer."

Sandi beamed from ear to ear.

"I want to call my buddy, Rhonda," Len said. "I'm thinking press conference."

Except for the prisoners' orange jumpsuits, everything was gray. Sandi had never been to a prison before, and she hoped she would never visit one again. Criminal law, while exciting and fast-paced was probably not the way she wanted to go. The prison experience was weird at best. She couldn't imagine what it would have been like to walk in here without Len on one side of her and Garrett on the other. Horrified by the undercurrent of tension and the vibration of anger that seemed to permeate the very air of the prison, Sandi felt the walls closing in. The feeling of dread at hearing those doors clang shut was punishment in the extreme.

They set up the camera in a cinderblock room with a gray steel door. No windows and fluorescent lights that probably never went off. Sandi was glad for the undergrad course in film and TV she'd taken as an elective. At least she knew how to set up the tripod when Garret pushed it at her, and she'd known how to check the lapel mic for levels. Once they had the video camera and the sound equipment in place, Len nodded to the guard, and a few moments later, a pale-faced Mark shambled in, taking his seat at the gray steel table. Garrett pulled focus and adjusted the bounce screen so that the fluorescent lighting was deflected a bit. When Garrett let her look through the view-finder, she noticed Mark's countenance had lost some of the greenish pallor that made him look so sickly when the guard brought him in.

Len stood off to the side, letting Garrett run the show. After a few jokes, Mark warmed up, and some of the tension seemed to drain from his eyes. They ran through a few different versions of his story. Garrett looked over to Len. "I got enough footage that I should be able to edit it into something useable. What do you think?"

"Let's take five and then we'll run through one more time from the beginning. Mark, this time try not to look away from the camera and keep your voice even and conversational. You want a mint, some water, maybe?"

Mark took in Len's words. "I could go for a drink, but it wouldn't be water." He laughed at his own joke.

Len unwrapped the end of a roll of lifesavers and showed it to the guard. When the guard nodded permission, he handed them to Mark, who popped a couple.

Mark cleared his throat. As the red light came on, he looked into the camera. "When I was a kid, my parents worked overseas for a while and we moved around a lot. But when my dad's health took a bad turn, we moved to D.C., and I went to school at Georgetown.

"After college, I started working as a courier. Those were the days before the internet, email, and other communication technologies made life easier." Mark rambled on. "I was good at languages, and pretty soon, word got around that I could speak Arabic. If somebody from one of the government agencies needed someone to deliver a package, I was the 'go-to guy.' Those were the jobs you used to hear about where you'd get on a plane, deliver a document, come back the next day, and get paid. I wasn't on the government payroll, for real, but you could call me an independent contractor. Most of the time I flew to Europe, but a few times I was sent to the Middle East."

Sandi let her mind wander, conjuring up an image of Mark in desert gear. In her imagination, a young Mark with a duffle bag slung over his shoulder, conferred with two men in kufiyahs and a black-robed mullah. Sandi pictured a whispered conversation and a trade-off between Mark and the mullah's henchmen.

Sandi whispered to Garrett, "I guess Fed Ex took over that niche."

Len's voice close by, interjected reality. "Mark, enough of this. Let's get back to the present."

"OK, sorry. Things changed. Reporters, investigations. Those jobs went away. Congress cleaned house, or so they claimed. Besides, I wanted a real career. I always had an interest in science so I went to graduate school and got a Ph.D. in microbiology."

"I was a graduate assistant to a well-known Georgetown professor, Mel Rudnik, who was head of the bio-hazards curriculum there. For two years, I practically ran the bio lab for him. In fact, while I was doing a post-doc, Vectelon provided the lab with a grant to work on a biotoxin project.

"After I got my PhD, I worked for a consulting firm for a couple of years. My first job with Vectelon had me managing one of their labs in Maryland. It was all above board. When the government talked about shutting down that contract for the anthrax vaccine, I got sent to the location where they were manufacturing the actual virus. Soon after I started working at the Manoaka reservation, I became aware of the dangerous working conditions and brought them to the attention of my boss. When he ignored me, I went over his head to the Vectelon corporate honchos about what was going on there."

"That was then. So why wait to talk now?" Len asked.

"What they were doing on the reservation wasn't right. They were endangering the lives of their employees." Mark held his head down, breaking eye contact with the camera. "Right away, I asked for more budget for safety equipment to cut down on workplace hazards. Maybe I could have been more discrete. In any event, my boss, Ken Daly, was super pissed. He couldn't fire me but he tried to get me to quit."

Len tried to stay upbeat but clearly, he was challenged. "But you've seen worse. Why get religion now?"

"True, I've seen worse. But, Vectelon? What they were doing was criminal." His voice trailed off until he seemed to pick up a thread. "After I left, I heard that two workers died from exposure to hazardous substances they came in contact with at the lab. The higher-ups' only response was to come in and vaccinate the workers. Had the work at Manoaka been done on U.S. soil, the rules on workplace hazards would have been mandatory. The company would have been liable for criminal prosecution.

"Maybe they still are," Sandi murmured.

Len yelled, "Cut." "OK, I think we have what we need. We're ready to go public with the whistleblower suit."

Garret turned off the cameras and stood down. Together, he and Sandi broke down the setup.

Sandi whispered, "I wish Mark could be there for the press conference."

"You wish?" Mark's voice was strained. "Len, what's the story? Can you get my bail lowered?"

"I'm working on it but something weird is going on," the lawyer said. "That's why the video is important. We're going to use it to go for the headlines."

"Headlines, I need more than that." Mark looked crestfallen. "I could rot in here. Like say I said, people in high places are pulling the strings. My wife left, took the kids, and moved back in with her folks. Says she's divorcing me. Vectelon is on my ass. You think all of this just happened? You gotta get me out."

Garrett pulled his car to the curb in front of Len's building. "I'll go through what we shot and try to make something out of it on a first edit," Garrett said. "Then you can take a look."

"Let me know when it's ready," Len said. His hand on the door, he was ready to head back into the building.

Sandi glanced at her watch as she extricated herself from the back seat. Thank God, it was almost five. Imagining the long hot shower that would wash the prison stink off her skin, she couldn't wait to get home.

Before they could open the brass door to the lobby, a slick-looking guy in a Sharkskin suit slid up to Len. "Len, baby, long time no see."

Len frowned, struggling to recognize the face in front of him. Failing that, he pulled back. "Do I know you?"

"You do now. Len Krause, you've been served." He slapped a subpoena in Len's hand and swiftly walked away.

CHAPTER
17

Seated with books on her lap, Sandi thought about trying to focus on the class assignment. Still, she found herself overwhelmed by the events of the last few days. She was so behind and tonight was the night she'd promised herself to complete her part of the chapter sections for the study group outline for Morgan's class. The deadline was looming. She knew if she failed to get it done, Ned might not be able to keep them from throwing her out of the group. At the sound of a knock on the door, she jumped and the notes spilled to the floor.

Sandi opened the door and Janine entered sheepishly. "Sorry, I'm late. We ran longer than I thought."

"How was it?"

"The new drummer is great. Plus, P.S., he's hot! We ran him through our playlist for this weekend. That's what took us so long. Did Emily go to sleep okay?"

"We played Candyland for a while. I made her hot chocolate and she went to sleep like a lamb." Sandi cracked the door of her bedroom. Inside, Emily slept soundly, covered by a quilt.

At the sound of voices, the child's eyes twitched open and Janine picked her up. "C'mon, Baby. Let's go home." She headed for the door. "Thanks, Sweetie. I owe you."

"Wait, I could use a favor."

Janine turned back. "Name it."

"The Vets for Peace rally is tomorrow at noon. It's going to be in the Square. Can you come? They need bodies."

"I'll pick her up after nursery school and we'll walk over."

"Don't forget, it's in Rittenhouse Square. Meet you near the fountain at noon."

Sandi hoped, come lunchtime, she'd be able to escape the office. Over the last few days, the tension was becoming more and more palpable. She had a sense that Dave was charged up about something. There were conversations she really didn't want to hear. The walls were hardly soundproof and she kept hearing words like 'money laundering' and 'indictment.' The angrier Dave got the calmer Len's voice became. For the hundredth time, Sandi wondered how the two of them could ever work together.

When looking for an escape, she'd retreated to the file room, happy to have something to do even if it meant copying mountains of subpoenaed documents. Still, harsh words carried down the hall.

Dave's bland demeanor seemed to have been transformed, replaced by a new persona. For what seemed like the third time in an hour, he'd bellowed at Len. "How could you have let this happen?"

Len kept his cool. "Don't you get it?"

"Yeah, I get it. You and your lowlife clients."

"Dave, chill the fuck out. This subpoena has nothing to do with you. Frankie Falcone got arrested again. Somebody's using him. Now he's pointing the finger at me."

"Well rest assured; I'm not talking to any grand jury."

"Trust me, they're fishing. It'll never get that far."

"You're in a dream world. You need a lawyer. If there's an indictment with your name on it, that's it."

Worried by what she'd heard, Sandi drifted out to the hall. Dave brushed past, jacket in hand, almost knocking her down. He barely paused on his way out the door.

Unsure what to do next, she walked back and forth to the supply room where boxed documents were stacked two deep. Dying to ask questions, but deciding to be discreet, she returned to her desk. When Len appeared, she let him know, "The documents are ready to go. Do you want to check them?"

"You followed the order list I gave you?"

Sandi nodded. "Got it all."

Len shrugged "I trust you. Just call the messenger service. Have them delivered to the courthouse."

Sandi dialed 1-800-LAWDOCS and drummed her fingers on the desk until customer service picked up. Once she had a confirmation number and a pick-up time for 2:30, she passed it on to the newly hired temp, who was catching up on the filing. Grabbing her jacket, she fled the building.

Outside, April was exploding onto the city streets. Winter had been mild this year. It almost seemed like winter had decided to skip the East Coast altogether. Most of the weather's fury went south, unleashing tornados in Alabama and along the Mississippi.

No matter what, the mild breeze felt lovely on her skin. Benches in the Square were filled to capacity, and a couple of guys leaned against the waist-high stone balustrades strumming guitars, doing their best to make their reed-thin voices heard above the clamor of midday traffic. Sandi's eye caught sight of Janine over by the play area, and she went to collect her friend.

"I brought some PB and J to keep Em quiet. Do you want one?" Janine offered a soggy purplish square. Sandi shook her head and pulled a yogurt from her bag. "No thanks, I brought this in case I get hungry." She gestured toward the edge of the park. "Shall we? It looks like they're setting up shop over there."

A Vets for Peace sign floated in the air near the park entrance on Nineteenth Street. A couple of guys in a mixed military kit of camouflage and jeans did their best to hand out flyers to passing throngs of workers in search of lunch.

Janine maneuvered the stroller off to the side, making room for the retirees, students, and shoppers who drifted by. She nudged her friend, and they exchanged satisfied glances as Emily's eyes fluttered closed and the four-year-old dozed off. "She loves nursery school but it tires her out."

Sandi checked her watch, hoping that they would start on time. She looked questioningly for Tony, soon spotting him just as he showed the group's parade permit to two cops in yellow vests, astride their bicycles. Finally, a tallish, mustachioed fifty-something in a Vets for Peace t-shirt stepped onto the platform. Moving closer, Sandi, Janine, and the sleeping Emily joined the few curious spectators who ambled over.

"Thank you all for coming out today. My name is Frank Berger. You might have heard my sportscast, The Sports Insider on WKIG-Radio. And today, I'm proud to announce the kick-off of our foundation supported by NFL and NBA athletes in support of our vets. We're here to support our troops but we're also here to call attention to what's happening to our vets. Also with us today is NFL vet, Barney Putnam." A brawny guy sporting an Eagles t-shirt under his camo jacket stepped up to the mic to the sound of applause and shouts of "Go, Putnam!"

"Before I share some exciting news, I'd like to tell you how I got here," said Putnam. "Just out of high school, I joined the military, and after serving my hitch, I was fortunate to be able to go to college using the GI benefits. Amazingly, I played college football and got drafted by the Seattle Seahawks. Then, a couple of years later, I joined the Eagles. After years on the field, I began to see similarities in the challenges that combat veterans and former professional athletes both face when they return to everyday life, and the uniforms come off.

"I'm here today to announce the funding of a rehab center and gym that we hope will provide both physical and mental therapy for our vets. We'll be breaking ground next week, and you're all invited. Be sure to listen in to Frank's show, The Sports Insider, for the time and place."

Frank stepped back to the mic with a smattering of applause. "Before I go any further, I want to introduce Tony Scott. Tony is just back from active duty."

There was light applause as Tony moved to the mic. "A lot of vets are suffering. They served their country. Now they're hurting, and they can't get help." As he took a breath, Frank jumped back in.

"Like Tony says, we have men back from active duty in the Middle East, both regular Army and reserves. We're hoping that our athletes working together with our vets can help them to put their lives back together."

"In many cases, we don't know everything that happened over there and the Pentagon is not providing much in the way of facts. What we do know is that there was an involuntary vaccination program, and we asked Senator Travino to investigate. He's promised to help, but he can't be here today, so Tony will be heading to Washington to meet with our reps in Congress. They don't seem to grasp the impact of what is happening to our vets. Some symptoms may be the result of a vaccine they were given. There's a possibility that others might be suffering from coming in contact with unknown substances when they were overseas."

Tony pulled out a poster board. Looking down at the hand-made graph, he pointed to a bar in red. "This shows the percentage of returned vets suffering from undiagnosed illness. The much smaller bar in green shows the number of returning vets who are receiving the treatment that they need. My aim is to put this information before the members of the Armed Services Committee."

Tony looked over, surprised, as Sandi stepped up to join him on the crowded platform. "I'm here because of my brother, Joe Brennan. He died serving his country. We were told that his death was caused by a landmine accident. But that wasn't true. It turned out that he was accidentally exposed to deadly toxins on the base of one of our own allies."

"Our troops face peril in battle but that's not all," Tony said as he looked at Sandi who nodded, gazing out at the crowd. "Our men and women have been exposed to harmful chemicals, biological toxins, and worse. And it's killing them."

Tony handed off the mic to Putnam. "Thousands have applied for benefits and have been turned down. Is it a cover-up or just plain ignorance? We want answers. Please call your congressman. Write to the newspapers. You just saw a few of the statistics. Take a flyer. For the bigger picture, go to our website, VetsforPeace.org."

Sandi and Tony stepped down from the platform. Janine gave Sandi a look and motioned her over.

Janine leaned closer, "The two guys who were standing behind me, did you notice?"

Sandi shook her head. "No."

"Giving off a weird vibe. When I looked around, the one had a tiny camera and it was pointed right at you two."

Seated in a conference room, poring over work papers, Greta had managed to ignore the muffled noise from the streets below until Ken Daly marched into the room. He headed to the window. "Have you seen this?" he roared. "They're here again.'

Greta shook her head. "No."

"Come here."

Obeying his command, Greta looked down. Seven floors below, five men and three women walked in an elongated circle before the entrance to the company headquarters. Their signs read, "Get off our land." "Your corporate profits are killing us."

"I'm sorry I missed it. I was trying to get this work done on schedule," Greta offered.

Down on the street, a young man with a bullhorn stepped out of the group. "Death mongers off our land." The group took up the chant which continued as a news crew arrived in a truck.

CHAPTER
18

With pillows to prop herself upright, Sandi stuck her feet out onto the coffee table. Since she'd lugged it home from the flea market, it had become her de facto desk, dining table, and footrest. Comfortable but determined, she was going to get some studying done. The semester would be over soon, and there'd be hell to pay if she didn't finish her chapters.

Out of habit, she flicked on the TV for company but kept the sound off. On-screen, Judge Judy seemed about ready to render a verdict on the hapless defendants before her. Sandi looked away and spent the next half hour outlining a short section of the Commercial Law text. The next time she raised her head, it was the local six o'clock news.

Uttering a cry of surprise, Sandi jumped up to get a better look at the screen. She saw a gaggle of reporters with mics outstretched, trailing Len, her boss, down the steps of the federal courthouse.

As she turned up the sound, she watched as Len slowed his pace, allowing a friendly TV reporter to ask, "Len, we heard Frankie Falcone implicated you in his testimony before the grand jury. Any comment?"

"Afraid I can't discuss that. Let's just call today's visit a fact-finding session."

"Any truth to the accusation of money laundering?"

"That's ridiculous. This thing will never go to trial. Have a great day, guys."

Heart racing, Sandi fought off the sense of dread that overtook her. She watched as Len gave a casual wave and walked out of the frame.

It was a rainy night in Washington. With the last of the cherry blossoms already gone, it was as though a button had been pushed, and spring had moved on, driven from memory by the invasion of heat and humidity that would cloak the city until November. Greta hoped that the rain would have washed most of the pollen from the air. Thank God they'd turned on the air in the building.

Stifling a yawn, Greta wondered why she was so tired. She could only hope that maybe tonight she might get some sleep. She tapped a lacquered fingernail on her glass desktop and took a final swipe at her screen. By accident, she pulled up that damned whistle-blower article, the one that accused Vectelon of selling biological toxins overseas, the one Ken Daly blew his top over.

She sighed as the last of her staff logged off of their computers and exited the building. She extracted Ken Daly's card key from her handbag hoping it was still good. He probably hadn't noticed it missing since he'd left for Phoenix that afternoon. She waited until the cleaning people had finished their floor. Then she scanned Ken's card at the door, making her way down the corridor toward the legal department file room. The room was dark, and she banged her shin on the corner of a long row of metal filing cabinets that faced each other across a three-foot aisle. The office manager kept talking about "going paperless" as though that could happen so easily. God knows how much time it would take to scan all of this paper. How many intern "man-hours" would it take, she wondered, just to finish even one bank of file drawers?

She flicked on her flashlight and moved the light up and down the cabinets until she found the one that read 'Export Licenses.'

Greta opened the drawer and pulled out a file. Moving to a table, she spread the pages flat before carefully focusing the high-quality miniature Minolta she bought just for the job.

She snapped every page in the extensive file and returned it to the drawer. Careful to leave no traces of her presence, she stacked each page carefully, returned the file to its rightful place, and pushed the drawer closed.

Greta returned to her desk. She opened the camera and pulled out the memory card, downloading the photos onto her laptop. She gave the file an innocuous name and uploaded everything to a flash drive. She took a padded mailing envelope from the drawer, addressing it carefully. After placing the camera's memory card in her handbag, she wrapped the flash drive in bubble wrap and dropped it into the mailer. The mailer went into her briefcase. She returned Daly's keycard to his desk drawer on her way out. Stepping onto the elevator, she pressed the down button. "Mission accomplished," she whispered.

Greta's footsteps rang out across the deserted lobby. She waved to the lone guard on duty.

"Night, Harry."

Greta looked over her shoulder as she moved toward the parking garage. The street was deserted, and the rain had stopped. Overhead, neon signs atop an office building glowed moonlike through the fog. Tops of the other tall buildings vanished in the haze. She was thankful that her car was on the first level and someone was still in the booth. She was getting a little spooked and wanted to get home. She pushed her card into the slot, and the gate flew up. Over the bridge, she was disappointed to find her local FedEx was already closed. Finding stamps in her briefcase, she added plenty of postage to the padded envelope before dropping it into the mailbox outside the Alexandria post office. Once that was done, she called Len, leaving a message when it went to voicemail. "Be on the lookout for what I just sent you. Lots of interesting reading. Should be there in a couple of days. Let's plan to meet on Wednesday at 6 a.m., same place. If you don't get the mailer before then, call me."

Greta was relieved to find parking half a block from home. From the trunk of the car, she retrieved her dry cleaning. Then, juggling briefcase in one hand, laptop in the other, and cleaning slung over her shoulder, she headed for home. "Almost there," she whispered to herself. Her back hurt. Could she force herself to eat something? Maybe she'd just skip the food and go to bed.

Greta turned her key in the lock. She flicked on the light in the hall and picked up the mail lying at her feet. She dropped her laptop and briefcase on the chair. The wilted fern on the hallstand next to the stairs silently pleaded for water. "Tomorrow," she promised. After making a mental note to water all the plants in the morning, she immediately forgot.

Kicking off her shoes, she carried them up the stairs. Fighting the urge to lay down on the unmade bed in her clothes, she pulled off her jacket and skirt. The blouse landed on the floor. She peeled off the offending pantyhose and rubbed her aching toes. Finding her sweats in the drawer, she pulled them on.

She looked around for the remote, thinking she might watch a few minutes of TV. "Try to have a life, why don't you?" she muttered aloud and laughed at herself. Looking in the mirror. she cricked her neck back and forth, watching as the muscles in her face and neck relaxed a little. But in a split second that relaxation is gone. From where she sat at the edge of the bed, she watched stunned, as the bedroom door slowly swung shut to reveal a gun with a silencer. The weapon was held by a man dressed in black turtleneck and jeans, baseball cap pulled low, obscuring his eyes. Greta's mouth formed a silent "O". Eyes wide, her hand reached out in a plea. Before she could speak, her words were silenced by the sound of two muffled shots. And Greta fell back across the pillows.

The gunman walked over to the bed. He felt for her pulse and then let her lifeless hand drop back onto her chest. Walking to the dresser, he picked up her jewelry case and emptied it on the bed next to the body. He sorted through a few pieces, causally holding one or two up to the light. With a shrug, he stuffed a handful in his pocket.

Downstairs, he found Greta's handbag on the chair and up-ended it on the upholstered seat. Emptying the wallet, he sifted through the contents as though looking for something. Uttering a muffled oath, he threw the handbag across the room. He then scooped up the briefcase and laptop, heading through to the kitchen. Seconds later, the rear door closed, and silence prevailed.

CHAPTER
19

Enjoying a few moments of quiet, Sandi took the morning's mail from the inbox and began separating what she took to be bills from the thinner envelopes that looked like they could be checks.

Using the letter opener, she placed the bills, still in their envelopes, into the appropriate folder marked 'Payable.' The checks, ready to be signed, were placed in a folder that she'd put on Len's desk. As a padded envelope caught her eye, she took note of an unfamiliar Virginia address.

She opened the brown envelope and pulled out its contents. There were several printed pages, along with an unlabeled flash drive at the bottom of the envelope. She slipped the drive into her desk drawer for safekeeping. Unfolding the top document, she was surprised by what she saw.

Manoaka Laboratories
A Vectelon Joint Venture

January 22, 2004

John Crough, CFO
Vectelon Corporation
1225 Dupont Circle
Washington, D.C.

Dear Mr. Crough,

The clearance documents were submitted for Manoaka Laboratories to the DoD and were found to be acceptable. They have been forwarded to you for your review and final legal approval.

The business plan that I received from the board also included a line-item budget, however, I should point out that this type of operation will require financing for precautionary measures at the highest level.

On February 15, 2004, I will be forwarding a unique list of agents and production techniques related to biological agents. As per your instructions, we will initiate manufacture on the reservation as soon as final approval is forthcoming. May I again stipulate that with biological materials of this type, the utmost caution must be exercised. This means increased financing will be necessary for hazmat materials and other safety equipment. Please see the attached for an itemized list of equipment awaiting budgetary approval.

Sincerely,

Mark Ricklin
Laboratory Manager

CC: Ken Daly

Sandi took the document to Len's office and put it on the top of his mail with a yellow sticky note attached. It read, "This just came in today's mail along with a flash drive I have in a locked drawer. Let me know if you want me to download the contents and print them out."

CHAPTER
20

After a last look around the battered Bridge Street storefront that was home to the Vets Center, Frank flicked off the light and locked the door. He pushed the final box of leaflets into the back of the battered pick-up parked at the curb. "That's the end of it."

Tony gave a silent thumbs-up as he closed the door.

"Driving straight through?" Frank asked.

Overhead, a train screeched on its way into the elevated station nearby and Tony waited for the noise to subside. "Crashing at my sister's place in Maryland. That'll give me a chance to spend a little time with her kids. Haven't seen them in a while. Should still be able to make it into D.C. on Wednesday, with some time before the rally."

"You got John's number, right?"

Tony nodded. "Gave him a call already. He's got me set up with a place to stay in D.C. Before the event, he says there's a reporter wants to interview me about our issue. And believe me, I am more than ready to talk."

"Good luck," Frank said. "Don't forget to keep me posted."

Tony hopped in the driver's seat and coaxed the engine to life. Finally able to gun it, he waved to Frank and pulled away. Heading south on Interstate 95, traffic was slow. More than a couple hours of driving stretched out before him. It was already past six. Tony told himself he could make do with the stops and starts of rush hour, but he only hoped he could get there before the kids went to bed. He didn't get to see them as much as he liked. Why hadn't he remembered to bring them something? Maybe he could pick up a little treat along the way, He loved the kids, and they knew it. If he could just stay in one place long enough to meet the right girl, he hoped for a family of his own. Tony tried to imagine what that would look like. But it was tough. For now, he didn't even have a real job much less a place to live. So, the family would have to wait.

Tony checked the radio traffic report, switched to an alt music station, got static, and turned it off. His nerves were shot. Since he'd gotten clean from the Adderall, he noticed that he had no patience. He'd never had any problems before they started adding the drug to the daily requirements of his recon team. The brass claimed it would make them sharper. They would be more alert, and more open to learning the physical and cultural lay of the land. But why? His team really hadn't even been in a combat zone. He continued to turn it over in his mind looking for answers.

The transition back to civilian life had been a tough one, but for now, what he was doing felt right. Even putting the unanswered questions of Joe's death aside, he still could not ignore the many other wrongs done to his fellow soldiers. His thoughts turned to the last time he'd spoken to Sandi and the crazy story she told him about seeing that lab on the reservation. It blew his mind. Sometimes it seemed like the enlisted men were becoming human guinea pigs for the many pharmaceutical and medical experiments that paid off big time to industrial concerns, almost like the prison experiments he'd read about in the old days. Before he left, everyone going to the Middle East was injected with a vaccine against anthrax. Would that have something to do with the strange metal containers Joe was exposed to? Maybe, maybe not? But there were a lot of questions he still had. Now that he was out of that world, he had a lot to wonder about. So many things didn't make sense until you tried to figure out who was benefiting from them; and where the profits were going.

As the miles unwound in front of him, Tony let himself be drawn into the highway's hypnotic spell. The monotony was already starting to drive him crazy. Before he left, he'd checked the route heading out of Philadelphia. Best just to stay on I-95, go around Towson, and then get on Route 70 to Hagerstown, where his sister Nancy and her husband Jack lived. By then, it would be past 8 o'clock, and the traffic would have started to die down. From there he could breeze through.

He stopped for coffee and grabbed a donut at the rest stop. Checking a map by the door, he traced the route with his finger. "How far to Hagerstown?" he asked the cashier. With a smile, she told him 44 miles.

By now, it was fully dark and the main street of Frederick was quiet. When he called his sister from there, her message picked up right away. He left his current location, asking if she could let the kids stay up a little longer.

Past the town limits, something drew his eye to the rearview. He'd noticed the two lights behind him when he got off at the exit, but they'd driven past when he stopped for gas. Now the same car was back and he wondered where it came from. Did they hide in wait behind a sign until he came through town? Tony shook his head, telling himself he was crazy. "You're nobody, man. Who are you kidding?"

He pushed buttons on the radio, again looking for some decent music with no luck. He wished he'd brought his own, but his MP3 player had died, and he wouldn't have the money for a new one until a job came through. Just as he saw the lights of Middletown up ahead, a tire blew and he cursed himself for being stupid. He should have checked the tires before. Even though he'd known he should get a completely new set, he'd rolled the dice.

Pumping the brakes, he pulled off the road toward a clearing in the tree line. He'd have to move all the stuff in the rear to get to his jack and the spare. He called Nancy again, and finally, she picked up, asking, "Where are you?"

"On the other side of Frederick, within spitting distance, but my tire blew. It's gonna slow me up so if the kids get tired, I'll just see them in the morning."

"OK, I've got some dinner waiting for you when you get here." Tony could hear a muffled voice in the background. "Jack says to tell you he's got a couple of beers for you too."

Tony cursed under his breath as he lifted two boxes of literature from the hatchback, looking for the electric jack he'd bought from the car's previous owner. He maneuvered everything out of the way so he could reach the spare in the tire well.

He'd just gotten the blown tire off when he saw a car moving toward him. "No damn street lights out here in the middle of nowhere," he muttered. By the time Tony registered that it was the same car coming back, it was too late to run. Squinting at the license plates, he watched two men emerge from within holding guns, their black hoodies making their faces unreadable in the dark. Shots rang out in unison.

As a tow truck pulled Tony's beat-up red pick-up into the impound lot, the lot attendant stuck his head out the window. "Whatta we got?" he asked the tow driver.

"This was off the road, over by Route 70 above Hagerstown. No driver around, but somebody left plenty of blood behind. I'd have said whoever was driving might have been a victim of road rage. But no sign of a body. Better call the cops. Whoever it was didn't make it. It's got New York plates. They'll have to track the registration."

Two days later, Frank stared at the fuzzy image on the battered TV set at the Vets Center. He pressed a button on the remote and ran the news clip back again, muttering under his breath. "I recorded the clip from CNN like they told me." He ran it back again, then pressed buttons on his cell. "Hey, John. Yeah, I got it recorded. But I don't see Tony nowhere. Didn't show? No way! He told me he was anxious to talk to that reporter. He left here on Monday. How could he not have got there by Wednesday?"

CHAPTER
21

Drum beats pounding in her ears, Sandi climbed stairs to the loft where Janine and the band rehearsed. Lucky for them, this rehearsal space was down by the river. In most neighborhoods, the police would have been called ages ago.

Spotting her friend come in the door, Janine danced over to where the guitarist played a riff. "Let's wrap it, guys." She pointed to a clock visible on the brick wall, the hands approaching eleven. "My ride's here."

The drumming stopped. "Thank God," Sandi murmured to herself.

The drummer disconnected the amps, and the band quickly broke down the equipment. "Anybody hungry? The Never Closed Diner is just two minutes away."

Janine took the mic off the stand and approached her friend. "Thanks for picking me up. Do you want to get something?"

Sandi wondered who might be watching Emily since that was usually her job. "Starving but don't you have to get home for Em?"

"No, I'm cool. Em's staying over at her grandmother's. So, for what it's worth, I'm a free woman for the night."

If only she could match their energy. Sandi felt out of place at the tag end of the high-spirited group making their way down the stairs. Out on the street, the night air failed to blow away her angst. Almost robotically, she followed the musicians as they headed toward a brightly lit diner sign, the deserted street's only illumination.

Janine hung back with her. "Why the long face? Study group no good?"

"It was a disaster. Everybody's pissed at me, even Ned. Can I blame them? I've been behind on finishing my share of the work all semester. I'd be pissed at me too."

"You've got a lot going on."

Sandi nodded. "Understatement of the year. I can't concentrate. I can't reach Tony. His phone goes right to message. My boss is in trouble and now the case I was working on…"

"Get something to eat. You'll feel better."

Inside the diner, two men at the counter nursed solitary cups of coffee. In a corner booth toward the rear, three men in suit jackets huddled, looking out of place in the gritty setting. One of them glanced out the window at the approaching group of noisy young people, and his eyebrows shot up. With a few words, he signaled to the others who, with studied casualness, skimmed their eyes over the group at the door. Sliding out of the booth, they all made their move to a side door. As they exited, one of the men put his head down in an effort to remain unseen.

As Sandi and Janine slid into a booth, Janine noticed Sandi's quizzical look. "What's going on? You look like you just saw a ghost."

Sandi, anxiety gripping her chest, frowned and waved her hand as if to clear a thought. "My imagination's working overtime. I could have sworn I just saw one of the lawyers I work for."

"You mean Len?" Janine asked.

"No, Dave, his partner."

"What would he be doing in a dump like this?"

"Yeah, you're right. I can't picture him being caught dead in a place like this."

The musicians, engrossed in their raucous humor, failed to register the presence of anyone except themselves. The waitress appeared with menus and after several minutes, they ordered. Waiting for the food to arrive, Janine nudged Sandi's shoulder. "C'mon, chill out. Forget about work for a change. Relax." Sandi gave her friend's arm a squeeze in acknowledgment of the advice.

Under a concrete bulwark close to the river, Len checked his watch repeatedly and dug out his cell. After punching in a number, he waited through several rings and then cursed as Greta's voicemail came up on the other end. At the beep, he tried hard to control his annoyance, but it came through, "Greta, I'm here waiting. You called me, remember? It was your idea to meet at the crack of dawn. Where the hell are you?"

He pocketed the phone and flipped on the radio. "Good morning, Delaware. Get out the umbrellas. It looks like some rain is headed our way, maybe even a windstorm this afternoon. And here's the breaking news ---" After ten more minutes, heaving a shrug that signaled dismissal, Len turned the key in the ignition, gunned the engine, and steered the car back up the embankment. He moved north, making his way back across the bridge. In his rearview, the words "Welcome to Delaware" faded from view.

Sandi, in jogging gear, exited her apartment building, bounding down the steps for an early run before work. At the bottom of the stairs, she looked at her watch, pondering her choice of directions. A pale sun skirted in and out of grey clouds, but the day promised to be warm. As she turned west, moving toward the greenery of the East River Drive, Sandi checked the intersection for oncoming traffic. Seeing none she moved between two parked cars, darted across the street, and broke into a jog, moving south. On Fairmount Avenue, traffic was light. Passing by the iron gates of the old Eastern Penitentiary, Sandi felt touched, as always, by the aura of gloom that emanated from its cold interior. Despite its recent revival as a tourist attraction, Sandi couldn't ignore the sad stories, the broken lives that these stone walls once held.

At a red light, she paused, taking a quick peek at her reflection in the mirrored windows of a bookshop. Breathing deeply, she hoped that her old friend, the runners high, would help her move from the dark place she'd been in for the last week. The only car in sight was a silver sedan half a block away. The light turned, and Sandi stepped off the curb. Increasing her pace, she tried to clear her mind of the anxiety she'd described to Janine the night before.

As she moved across the street, the silver car sped up, hurtling toward her. Why did the car feel like a weapon? If she didn't know better, she'd think they were coming for her. Was she the target? She peered into the car, registering the faces of two men staring at her from behind the windshield. In a moment of realization, she whispered, "Joe, help me. I've got to find Len."

Sandi made a 90-degree turn and ran in the opposite direction down the one-way street. Attempting to follow her, the goons in the silver car turned the wrong way into oncoming traffic. Horns blared as a taxi skidded into their path, blocking them. To avoid a head-on collision, the cab swerved, jumped the curb, and hit a pole. The driver, a hefty-looking man in a turban, extracted himself from behind the wheel. From the sidewalk, he shouted, "What you have done, you no-good bastards. I will kill you."

He turned to the only passers-by, a mother herding her children to the elementary school a block away. "Did you see that? Did you see what they do? They run me off the road." He flipped open his phone. "I call the police." The car backed away from the ruined cab and turned again to follow Sandi.

Sandi ran on, down a narrow alley where a parked truck blocked the way of any through traffic. Ducking behind it, she watched as the car slowed, stopped and, then continued past the alley. Sandi exhaled, then realized that they could go around the block and come at her from the other direction. She changed her path then, huddling in the shadowed doorway of an abandoned church. Peering around the corner, she saw her way clear to change direction, moving away from the taxi, away from the river, leaving its vulnerable open spaces behind. Instead, she would run toward the Philadelphia skyline seeking refuge in the increasing numbers of pedestrians populating the sidewalk as the clock moved closer to the morning rush hour.

Len's Porsche tore up I-95, moving north. Past the airport, he took the off-ramp labeled Center City Philadelphia. Despite the early hour, traffic slowed to a crawl. The morning drive-time announcer warned, "Watch out for the back-up at Pattison Avenue."

"Yeah, right." Len did a slow burn as he inched the Porsche forward. While a fire truck approached with lights and sirens, rubberneckers crawled past a tow truck as it extricated a wrecked SUV from the rear of a panel truck. Two cops took the drivers' statements on the side of the road. From the look of things, nobody seemed to be injured. Finally, the lane opened up, and he was able to make the turn, breaking free of the congestion.

Minutes later, Juan greeted him at the entrance to the parking lot with an elaborate bow. "Good morning, my friend. How are you?"

"Tired and pissed, I got up at 4:30 to meet with someone who didn't show."

"You do look a little off your game. I know how it is. Not enough sleep, too many late nights?" He gave a wink.

"I wish." They high-fived with Len cracking a smile.

"Well, you may be beat, but your car," Juan kissed his fingertips. "She looks beautiful."

Len gave a thumbs-up. "Later, my man." He gunned the engine, shifting gears as the car screeched up the ramp. Recalling a forecast for rain and the possibility of hale, he decided to forego his usual spot on the top floor, pulling into a protected area in the corner. The sign read: YOU ARE AT LEVEL 4.

Still in her jogging clothes, Sandi moved past the parking lot, focusing on the office building half a block away. Entering the lobby, she planted herself in front of the building concierge who sat, with eyes closed in front of the console. When Sandi gave a polite cough, he opened one eye. Seeing her he broke into a welcoming smile.

"Len in yet?" she asked.

"Nope, haven't seen him?"

In need of a sympathetic ear, Sandi stopped to catch her breath. "You wouldn't believe what just happened. A car tried to run me over."

The concierge nodded, making sympathetic sounds of agreement. "I hear you. The way people drive today is a sin."

"No, I mean, they really tried to kill me."

"That's like what happened to me and the missus. We were at the mall, in the parking lot and this Jersey driver comes barreling…"

Sandi tuned him out, transferring her attention to the front entrance, her gaze riveted on two men in suits pushing through the revolving door. As the pair walked past her toward the elevators, they gave her pink sweats questioning looks before turning away. Watching them push the "up" button to summon the car, she relaxed. Pacing back and forth, she waited for Len to appear. After what felt like an eternity, she bolted the building, deciding to check the parking lot.

At the entrance, she spotted Juan leaning in the driver's side window of a stalled green station wagon blocking the main entrance. Backing up in the street behind, irritated regulars, waiting to take possession of their pre-paid parking spots, blasted annoyance through their horns. Sandi peered in at the woman behind the wheel.

Looking distraught, the woman repeatedly turned the key in the ignition. Each time, the engine sputtered and died. Juan walked around the car. He leaned back into the driver's side window. "Why don't you slide over and let me give it a try?" As though she hadn't heard the question, the woman continued her silent refusal to abandon her futile strategy. Exasperated, he shook his head, gesturing to the driver next in line.

As Sandi ran past Juan, she realized that getting his attention was hopeless. His morning had disintegrated into a shouting contest as he tried to appease angry regulars who cursed him as they waited to park. Idling cars lined both sides of the narrow street, creating a traffic jam of epic proportion that extended around the corner. And still, inexplicably, the woman sat immobile, refusing Juan's help. Normally she would feel some solidarity with a fellow woman driver bearing the brunt of male road rage, but not today. Sandi wondered if, for once in his young life, Juan might actually have wished for a cop to appear and extricate him from this disaster.

Sandi headed to the elevator and pressed the button. LED lights overhead signaled the car's slow descent. The doors opened to reveal a young mother with her toddler son in a massive stroller. As the woman navigated the baby carriage out of the elevator, its young passenger let out a howl.

"Burpy, Burpy!" His plaintive cries shredded the quiet as he stretched out his arm to retrieve a blue terrycloth plaything lying on the elevator floor.

"Oh, Jeffy. You dropped Burpy again?"

Seemingly satisfied that he had gotten his mother's attention, the child stopped crying and smiled. As his mother wiggled past him to retrieve the dropped toy, the toddler stood up in his seat and happily pushed the button for every floor on the elevator control panel. Satisfied, he beamed at Sandi and plunked his well-padded rear back onto the stroller seat.

"Look." The mother showed Jeffy the retrieved plaything. "Burpy is all dirty. I have to wash him before you can play with him again."

Reaching out, Jeffy whined for his lost treasure as his mother trundled him off without so much as an apologetic glance in Sandi's direction.

Sandi entered the elevator. "Finally." At Level 2, the doors opened and closed several times. "Goddammit." She pushed the "Door Close" button over and over. Giving up on the elevator, she jumped out and headed to the stairwell. Intuition and the sound of voices below drew her to look over the concrete barrier down into the back alley. Moving around a dumpster at street level, she spotted two men, noticing their close-cropped hair, and their round faces. Could they be the ones who came after her in the car? As one pulled open the door to the back stairwell, the other motioned for him to stop. The second man pulled something from inside his suit jacket but Sandi was unable to see what it was. With a new sense of urgency, Sandi charged up the stairs, hoping to find Len on Level 7 before they did.

Len's briefcase sat open on the passenger seat inside the Porsche parked on Level 4. Next to it, an empty coffee mug sat in the cup holder. Len finished organizing his documents in a folder and snapped the case shut. With annoyance, he noticed the cup had tipped the few remaining drops of coffee onto the car's immaculate floor mats. "Goddammit," he swore, reaching down to swab up the offending liquid.

As he righted himself, a shadow fell over the interior of the driver's side. Len turned to see a man in sunglasses, holding a gun aimed point blank at his chest. Making a brash attempt to push the gun away, Len grabbed for the barrel. As the gun fired, Len fell back across the seat. In his final moments on earth, Len watched as the man wiped the gun, removed the silencer, dropped it in his pocket, and placed the gun in Len's lifeless fingers, closing them around the weapon. The shooter again reached into the car's interior and extracted the lawyer's briefcase. Wordlessly, he motioned to his accomplice standing guard mid-point between the elevator and the stairwell. Together the pair walked calmly down the exit ramp.

Sandi arrived on Level 7. Surprised that Len's car was not in its usual spot, she ran to the elevator that now waited, door open, on the seventh floor. Running in she hit the button for 6. It stopped. Holdings the door open, she peered out. No Porsche. She repeated the exercise on Level 5. Arriving at Level 4, she spotted Len's car nestled in the corner; the front end turned toward the concrete wall.

The car looked empty. Why would Len have parked there? Sand whispered to herself, "Len, where are you?"

Down at street level, Juan still tried to reconcile the traffic nightmare. Spotting two men walking down the exit ramp, he did a double-take. He didn't recognize them as customers, but one carried a briefcase that looked strangely familiar. He squinted at it, trying to make out the initials. Moving past the stalled green station wagon that still blocked the entrance, the pair exited the lot and disappeared into the street.

As if on cue, the driver at the wheel of the stalled, green car checked her watch and looked into the rearview mirror. She turned the key in the ignition. Miraculously, the engine purred smoothly to life. With a smile and a wave to Juan, she backed out of the lot. "Changed my mind. Thanks anyway." Dumbfounded, Juan watched as the car pulled away and turned the corner.

On Level 4, Sandi spotted Len's car. Running toward the Porsche, she called out his name, but she was unable to get closer. Blocking her way, a blue Toyota moved toward the space next to Len's car and the driver began a lengthy and awkward K-turn maneuver. After what felt like forever, the strange parking operation ended with the blue car's front end facing out.

Exiting her car, the female driver peered into the Porsche next to her. In horror, she screamed. "Oh, my God. Help, help…" She gestured wildly before collapsing on the hood of her car.

Sandi moved around to the driver's side of Len's car. Opening the door, she was horrified by the blood-spattered interior. "Oh, no. No! Len. Len." Fighting off the terror at seeing his body slumped to the side, she reached for Len's wrist. Sensing no pulse, she looked around shocked and dazed.

Seeing the Toyota driver slumped against the hood of her car in a faint, Sandi reached into the Toyota, blasting the horn. She turned to the driver, "For God's sake, call the police."

Searching in her handbag, the woman produced a phone. With hands shaking, she punched 9-1-1 and silently held it out to Sandi who grabbed it away from her. "Help," she cried into the phone. "I'm at the Shurfine Parking Garage. My boss has been shot."

"What's the location, ma'am?" The dispatcher interjected.

"It's on the 4th level."

"I understand, Ma'am, but where is the garage located? What street?"

"It's on Spruce, 18th, and Spruce."

"OK. A car is on the way."

Sandi dropped the phone and turned to the witness. "What did you see?"

"I just pulled in. I only saw the car. I was parking." The woman sobbed, "Trying not to be late for work, I didn't see…"

Leaving the distraught woman in tears behind her, Sandi ran down the ramp, barely avoiding two screeching cars, the drivers half-crazed by their long wait. At street level, she found a harassed-looking Juan, waving cars into the lot. His eyes asked a question. Sandi, distraught, beat on his chest with a command. "Call an ambulance. Len's been shot. Tell the police to go to Level Four."

Oblivious to the drama, pedestrians walked by. Across the street, Sandi spied Garrett. With his head down, the private investigator walked and talked, his attention given over to the conversation emanating from his headphones. Tires screeched as Sandi ran in front of a car, almost becoming a traffic statistic herself. As she pulled the bud from his ear, a startled Garrett jumped. "What's going on?"

"They shot him."

"Shot who?"

"Len. They shot Len. In his car."

A siren sounded in the distance. As a squad car arrived, she turned away, running back across the street. Seeing her at the passenger side door of the police cruiser, the driver waved her around to his side. Just then, Juan ran over. "Shooting up above." He pointed.

"How many?" The cop asked.

"My boss," Sandi said. "Len, they shot him."

The cop picked up the radio. "Unit 67 requesting back-up and an ambulance. Location, Shurfine Parking, 18th and Spruce."

As Sandi jumped into the front seat of the patrol car, Garrett asked permission with his eyes. The cop nodded, and the private investigator slid into the back. A dazed-looking Juan watched the squad car screech up the ramp.

On Level Four, the sobbing woman had pulled her car away from the Porsche into a far corner. As sirens announced the approach of backup, a police car blocked the entrance to Level Four. When a second car arrived, Cop One pointed to the lifeless body behind the wheel. Then he nodded toward the woman in the blue Toyota.

"She our witness?" Cop Two asked.

The weeping woman, silent behind the wheel, got out of the car and moved warily toward the cops standing near the Porsche. Sandi wanted to scream as she heard the woman blubber to the cop about being fired if she was late again.

"Sorry, ma'am, but you'll need to stay here and provide some information about what you saw. We need your help. Try to keep calm. Was there anyone here when you arrived?" the policeman asked.

"Her. I saw her!" She pointed to Sandi.

"Where did you see her?"

"She got off the elevator and ran to the car. Then she started screaming at me."

The cop looked at Sandi hovering nearby.

"I wanted to tell him. I tried to tell him."

The second cop asked, "Is it a robbery, a hit? Anything missing, money, jewelry?"

Garrett asked, "Is there a weapon around?"

The cop looked down. "Here's the gun in his hand. What gives?"

More police officers arrived at the top of the ramp. Down below, two officers directed traffic. The elevator doors opened, and paramedics emerged with packs and a portable gurney.

The cops made way for the EMTs to check the body. "Too late for this guy," the paramedic announced. "Call forensics."

Hearing those words, Sandi's heart stopped.

Running interference. Garrett moved next to Sandi. He told the cop, "The victim and I had a meeting set up for this morning."

Sandi turned to Garrett. "Somebody tried to run me over. I came to find Len, to tell him to be careful. Why won't anybody listen to me?"

"We were too late," said Garrett. "This is bizarre. The timing is super weird."

"What do you mean?" Sandi asked.

"The press conference on Mark Ricklin and Vectelon? Len scheduled it for tomorrow. Len planned to announce the filing of Mark's whistleblower suit against Vectelon.

CHAPTER
22

Inside a hotel conference room, a podium with multiple microphones faced out on fifty chairs arranged theater style. In the rear, Garrett stood at the door. Nearby, Sandi was ready to hand out press releases and a synopsis of the research on Vectelon and Len's client, Mark Ricklin. When the first journalist arrived, it was someone Garrett knew. In low tones, Sandi could hear him describe the sad events of the last few days. In contrast, Len's partner, Dave, seemed to be squelching any and all questions from a local TV news reporter. As Sandi moved closer, trying to hear what he was saying, the lawyer swept the journalist out of the room.

Two men in jeans entered and took the handouts on offer. Dave re-entered, bringing the hotel manager with him. Rhoda, Len's publicist, all bright copper hair, wearing a sharply tailored suit, trailed behind. Sandi tried to grab Rhoda. "Did you invite the guys from Vets for Peace like I asked? They should be here."

Planting her tortoiseshell glasses firmly on her head, Rhoda shrugged and her face told the story. Sandi said, "I take that as a no." As she surged forward, angrily, Garrett pulled her back.

Dave stepped to the podium, and the room fell silent. "Ladies and gentlemen, thanks for coming today but I'm afraid that I have some very sad news. I'm sorry to announce that my partner, Len Krause has met with a tragic accident." Making no secret of his intention to shut down the proceedings, he continued. "I'm sorry but we won't be continuing with the press conference. Our firm has resigned the case and is no longer representing Mr. Ricklin." Dave turned to Rhoda as he moved away from the microphone.

Looking around, there were a few raised hands. A young man in jeans shouted out, "Can you tell us what happened?" Amid the confusion, Rhoda urged Dave to respond to the buzz in the room,

Dave moved back to the mic. "As soon as we know more, we'll be able to make a statement. This press conference is canceled." A young woman and a cameraman had just finished their setup out in the hall. They looked at each other in surprise.

Sandi's head and heart made a dive into a black pit of despair. Feeling dizzy, she grabbed the back of a chair and waited for the room to come back into focus. Dave strode past with the hotel manager, who gave the nod, signaling two hotel employees.

Sandi grabbed Dave's sleeve. "Dave, please. Don't do this."

"Don't do what?" His eyes were dark and cold. He shook off her touch.

"But we're ready. We have the information."

"We? Who is we?"

"What I meant to say is…"

"It doesn't matter now. Didn't you hear what I said? The firm no longer represents Mark Ricklin."

As the lights dimmed, Sandi ran to the rear where Garrett was engaged with a reporter. Before she could supply the details of yesterday's events, the reporter took a call. Seconds later, he motioned to a photographer. "Let's go."

"Wait, please. Let me tell you what happened."

As the two men pulled their gear together, she held out some papers.

"Bank robbery and a shooting out on City Line Avenue. The boss wants a photo for page one. Let's go."

"Can't you at least take this?" She offered a sheaf of papers to the reporter who obliged and stuffed them in his pocket. Still, the body language told her that she had lost them. They'd already moved on to the next story.

Dave was now out in the corridor. Sandi watched him glad-hand the remaining press out of the room as they shut it down. He looked over his shoulder and whispered to Rhoda.

With a big smile, she approached Sandi. "Here, sweetheart. Let me help you with those." They engaged in a tug of war as Rhoda took control of the handouts.

The week-end followed sticky for early May. In her mind, Sandi walled off the events of the last week. She told herself that the time she spent studying for her final exams had kept her from going insane. With a ferocity that amazed her, she had attacked the law books and the notes that she previously hadn't had time for.

Her heart was heavy but she could hear Joe's voice in her head. "C'mon, Sandi, you gotta try." She answered him aloud. "How can I get through this?"

On the verge of losing a whole semester as she was, she again fell back on Ned who sacrificed some of his own study time to help her. After they'd studied through the night, Ned still dozed on her loveseat. At the sound of Sandi's voice, his eyes fluttered open. "What? What did you say?'

"Just talking to myself."

He looked at his watch. "OK, let's get busy. We still have three hours before the exam."

"Thanks, Ned. You are saving my life."

Hours later, standing outside the law school building on Temple's campus, Sandi waited silently for Ned to emerge from the test room. She gritted her teeth, listening to her classmates, the ones with the highest grade-point averages, asking each other about the answer to this or that question. She tried to ignore them as they stood around, telling each other how badly they had done on the test.

Sweating despite a shiver in her heart, Sandi stood apart. How things had changed. She'd gone from being a carefree student whose only fears were paying the rent, and worrying about her student loans. Most of the time her biggest concern had been what she was going to do over the week-end. Now, she felt old.

The air felt gritty and thick. Summer had descended on the city of Philadelphia like a heavy cloud.

A passerby complained, "What gives? We go from winter to summer in a week-end."

His buddy answered, "I hear you. Could be global warming. Could be them scientists messing with the sky. The Chinese shooting stuff into the clouds, trying to change it up…control the weather."

"Yeah, like they try to control everything else."

Near the curb, she spied the stack of newspapers inside the box for the Daily News. Reading the headline made her feel faint. "Police Call Lawyer Death Suicide."

As always, the concierge saluted Sandi at the door. After signing for a delivery, he pointed the UPS driver toward the freight elevator. Then, a Fed Ex package arrived. Unable to chat, but still glad to see her, he smiled. Across the corridor, Sandi pushed the elevator button that would take her to the sixth floor. Looking around, everything looked the same, yet it all felt so different.

And it didn't just feel different. It was different. On floor six, the door to the law office of Krause and Nielsen stood open as the old signage was being removed. Sandi slipped across the office threshold glad she didn't have to worry about being buzzed in. From behind the reception desk, a fresh-faced Asian beauty asked, "How may I help you?"

Sandi pointed to the little desk in the corner. "I used to work here. My things are here, I just came to get them."

"Oh." The countenance changed. "Just a minute. I cleaned those drawers out. Let me get that box for you." She stood, smoothing nonexistent wrinkles from her dress, and headed into the file room.

Down the hall, Sandi heard Dave, "OK, Sam, see you at the club at one." Coming from Len's office, as it did, the sound jarred her.

The receptionist wordlessly offered Sandi a small cardboard carton. Sandi peeked into the box and was surprised to see the black flash drive that had come in the mail that day.... the day before everything turned awful. She remembered that it had come in the envelope with an Alexandria postmark. She palmed the flash drive into her pocket, moving past the new girl down the hall to Len's office where Dave now sat, with his feet up on the desk. At the sight of her, his posture changed. His feet swooped to the floor, and he pulled himself erect, trying to look forbidding, she thought.

Reception Girl stood at the door wearing an apologetic expression. As Dave waved her away, she backed out. Sandi offered the box to Dave for inspection. "Just wanted you to know I'm taking nothing but what I came in with."

"No problem. Good luck with everything." He extended a hand in a half-hearted gesture of goodwill, but

Sandi ignored it. At that, Dave stood, moving forward as if to maneuver Sandi out the door.

"Are you surprised by what the papers printed about the way Len died?" she asked.

Dave bristled. "My partner had dealings with the wrong kinds of people."

"What are you saying?"

"I'm talking about a criminal element. You sleep with dogs you get up with fleas."

"What does that mean?"

"Len was about to be indicted. He knew his name was in the mud."

"I don't believe it!"

"Face it. His career was shot. Len knew it. He took his own life."

"No! No, he didn't. That's a lie."

Dave moved back around his desk. "That's what the investigation found and that's what they wrote."

"No, that's what you told them."

Dave changed his mind. Now the look on his face was one of menace. His body forced her toward the door, and she backed out to the hall. "Just so you know, I called a reporter from the press conference," Sandi said.

"Really? Will they be printing a retraction?" Dave's tone was mocking. As they reached the main office door, Dave jostled the sign guy aside. Maneuvering Sandi out through the entryway into the hall, he slammed the door shut.

CHAPTER
23

Sandi perched on the edge of a small slipper chair inside the Civil War-era farmhouse in West Virginia. Outside, the birds sang a full-throated ballad to a summer evening. The pines exuded a woodsy fragrance as the shadows grew longer. Despite the higher altitude, the air here seemed richer and fuller. There was more of it.

Dr. Haynes seemed less formidable now in jeans and a sleeveless t-shirt with her dark hair pulled back in a ponytail. Still, as she peered out over the glasses that had slipped down to the end of her nose, Sandi had trouble explaining what it was she wanted to say.

Instead, Sandi held out copies of documents she'd assembled. "The ones in the blue folder came from one of the lab trucks from the reservation. The second set, in the red folder, came from Vectelon's internal records. They were mailed to my boss by somebody from the company, but he never got a chance to read them before he was killed."

"I'll take a look," said Haynes. "But I'm not sure how relevant they'll be now that it's gone."

"What's gone?"

"The lab's gone. Cleaned out, shut down."

"Yes, I heard that might happen. We were working on a case, a whistleblower suit. Trying to show what they were doing there. The private investigator I was working with had been in touch with a reporter on the Manoaka paper. Maybe you know him? His name's Jesse. If it wasn't for what Jesse told us, we wouldn't have known to get in touch with you.

"Right from the beginning, I knew something was wrong there," Haynes said. "Especially after I heard what kind of company they were working with. After two of the workers died under strange circumstances, Vectelon wanted to come in and vaccinate every member of the tribe. The tribal leader wouldn't agree to it, but they did succeed in vaccinating all the employees who worked in the lab. Their families, too, as I remember. I have a friend in Indian Affairs in D.C. I told him what happened on the reservation, but when he asked me for details; about what they were doing there, sadly, I had no proof."

"But that's what I want to show you. It's a P.O. for a shipment of bioagents to Saudi Arabia. When I showed it to Garrett, the investigator I'm working with, he called it the smoking gun."

"Where did you get this purchase order?" Haynes asked.

"This might sound crazy, but I snitched the copy of a purchase order out of a Vectelon van. Then there was a flash drive with files from the company that came in the mail. Len left me a message to print out everything that was on the drive. But it was late in the day, and I put it off. It was only later, after his death, that I was able to retrieve it. When I printed out everything on the flash drive, the documents were a paper trail that led from the company headquarters to the Manoaka lab to sales of biological materials overseas."

"I have a meeting with the head of the Manoaka Reservation tomorrow," Haynes said. "May I make a copy of this memo from Mark and the Manoaka purchase order and show it to him? I doubt that he's aware of all of this."

"Yes, you're welcome to take the whole file but, if you don't mind, I'd like to be there with you."

"We weren't planning to talk about the lab. The purpose of the meeting is to go over the health regulations before the grand opening of their new casino. But seeing this, I don't think we should sit on it," said Dr. Haynes.

The next day, after the casino meeting, Dr. Haynes introduced Sandi to Andy Russell, also known as Grey Owl, chief of the Manoaka Nation. "I know this is a lot to take in and I know that the Manoaka people have suffered greatly at the hands of Vectelon Corporation and what they did on your land," Sandi said. "My boss, Len Krause, had a client who was managing the laboratory, Mark Ricklin. He was ready to file a whistle-blower complaint. The firm was trying to get proof of the crimes being committed."

"Why didn't they come to me?" the chief asked. "Ricklin wasn't here that long. Maybe a couple of weeks.

Still, he knew who I was. We'd met in my office, the day he started. He knew where to find me."

"I don't have the answer to that, but he should have. Things happened fast. Soon after Ricklin left the lab, he was arrested on an unrelated drug charge. He's been behind bars ever since. There was a press conference scheduled with plans to report what was going on. But the day before, Len Krause, Ricklin's lawyer was murdered and the press conference was canceled."

Dr. Haynes and the Manoaka chief exchanged looks "Thank the Great Spirit, they've gone from our land, taking their evil poison with them," Grey Owl said.

After the leader listened carefully to what she had to say, Sandi was surprised to hear Grey Owl say he wanted to know more, he wanted her to continue the investigation. "Truth is needed to cleanse our tribe," he said.

"Where can we start?" Sandi asked. "I would be more than willing to talk to any tribe member who might have something to share. But how can we find them?"

"I can give you names of the tribe members who worked in the lab, and I believe that there are also a few local people, like the truck drivers who were on the payroll," Grey Owl said. "They wouldn't be members of the tribe, but they might know something."

"But how could we find them?" Sandi asked.

"Maybe we could advertise? Put an ad in the local paper? Wait! I know. How about a billboard?' said the chief's assistant, rattling off some ideas.

Sandi and Dr. Haynes exchanged glances but kept silent.

"I like that. The tribe will pay for the billboard, but first, you must help us decide what will be on it," said Grey Owl.

Dr. Haynes, Grey Owl, his assistant, and Sandi spent time going back and forth deciding what the billboard might say. "If our tribe could afford it, I would offer a reward," Grey Owl said. Finally, the chief gave Sandi permission to ask the only question she wanted answered.

"Is there any other way I can help?" Sandi asked.

"You and Dr. Haynes know more about the situation than anyone else," the chief said.

"I know Dr. Haynes doesn't have the time, but I would be more than willing to stay here and talk to anyone who can shed light on what happened."

Soon after their meeting, the chief provided Sandi with a cell phone whose number would appear on the billboard in large print. Wondering how she could afford to stay nearby; Sandi was excited when Dr. Haynes offered her the use of her guest room for a few days while she stayed to interview people on the reservation.

Three weeks later, the shiny new casino opened, and as word spread, people began to find their way to the Manoaka Reservation. Before they made the turnoff that would take them to the casino, they couldn't help but drive by a billboard that asked the question, "Who Killed Len Krause?" Anyone with information about the case was asked to call a local number. Sandi hoped the calls might shed some new light on the mystery.

Appearing, as it did, on a sparsely trafficked stretch of road half a mile from the entrance of the new casino, the calls about the billboard were so few that Sandi wondered if anyone had even seen it. Yet, as word of the new casino spread, highway traffic picked up and the curiosity about the cryptic question on the billboard grew. No one really knew who Len Krause was but some local people who had worked at the lab were curious to know more about what happened.

Excited by the interest, Jesse used it for the lead headline on a Monday edition of the Manoaka Courier. Though no one was able to answer the cryptic question, the story spread, picked up by the local TV news. Soon after, buzz spread to the Washington Post, with a Post headline reading, Lawyer's Death Provokes Mystery.

CHAPTER
24

Quivering with a mixture of excitement, awe, and vindication, Sandi could have pinched herself as she looked around the richly paneled Congressional hearing room. A panel of four Congressional committee members faced them across the wooden dais. Dr Haynes sat at the draped table with the tribal elders. In front of them, four photographers, two male and two female, in jeans and boots, crouched on the floor, cameras trained on those who would be answering the day's questions. The flashes came in a burst and then subsided at the sound of the gavel striking three times.

Sandi wondered if things went well, would a discussion of Mark's situation create a call for further investigation? Would the whistleblower have a chance to tell what he knew? If so, there would almost have to be a new hearing. Could Mark be released from prison? Unfortunately, he still had the drug charges to contend with.

Even though she wasn't scheduled to testify; Sandi believed that she knew much of what the witnesses might be called upon to share. As the meeting came to order, she turned in her seat, giving Garrett, sitting two rows back, a pointed smile. Across the aisle, the Vectelon attorneys made up a phalanx of antagonism, their faces stony with enmity.

The committee chair, Congressman Clark of Oklahoma, led the proceedings. "As chairman of the House Committee on Indian Affairs and as the representative of the great state of Oklahoma, I welcome the members of the Manoaka Nation to our chambers. Congressman Tyler, on behalf of the great state of West Virginia, would you like to make an opening statement to your neighbors and constituents?"

Indicating his desire to speak, Congressman Tyler cleared his throat before turning to the camera with a smile.

"As a Congressional representative of a state that has struggled with towering levels of unemployment, I've made it my life's work to bring job opportunities to our state. As you may recall the Tyler Mailing Center provided 500 jobs once it was built and open."

Minutes later, Sandi and Dr. Haynes exchanged looks of satisfaction as Grey Owl, chief of the Manoaka Nation, leaned into the microphone to begin his testimony. "For this Congressional hearing, let this testimony serve to provide the history of the Manoaka Tribe, resident on our land for many hundreds of years. Up until the last fifty years or so, the state of West Virginia claimed that there were no indigenous tribes living in our state. As the current vice president of the Appalachian American Indian Foundation, I want to set the record straight. Our goal has been to bring our people together, to help them make contact with our history and our heritage, and to achieve recognition.

"The Manoaka have lived on our land since before the first settlers landed at Jamestown. At that time our tribe numbered perhaps more than 3000 people. In addition to hunting for food, many members of the tribe lived by growing corn, beans, and squash. Today the tribe still numbers over a thousand people, some of whom live on the reservation while others live on tribal lands that we've purchased on Deer Mountain. The tribe became a state-registered entity that has continued to purchase parcels of land for our members on the mountain and surrounding areas and we are dedicated to the economic survival of our tribe.

"Vectelon first came to us several years ago, asking us to partner with them. I believe it was in 1998. They told us that we would receive training and jobs in a high-tech field. Our people would benefit from what they called 'marketable skills.' Yes, I believe that was the phrase they used. It was in this spirit of survival that the tribe entered into a partnership with Vectelon Corporation. According to our agreement, the company promised to provide income for leasing the land and also jobs and training for our people. We gave them permission to build the laboratory and train our people to work there. Unfortunately, the jobs they gave us were deadly."

"Too late, we found that Vectelon only sought us out to take advantage of our reservation status as an independent sovereign entity. Their purpose was to test, produce, and sell harmful biological materials that were not permitted to be manufactured on American soil. Because of dangerous working conditions, they were responsible for the deaths of some of our tribe members. In light of these activities, the tribe has broken all connections with the corporation. We have now turned our economic interests to the creation of a casino and entertainment complex on the West Virginia southern border, near Blue Run Creek."

Once he'd gotten that into the Congressional record, the tribal leader was ready to move on to the issue at hand, the tribe's abuse by Vectelon Corporation.

"You say the jobs they gave to your tribe were deadly?" Tyler asked. "Can you tell us more?"

Placing his hand over the mic, Grey Owl's attorney whispered in his ear and the chief nodded. "If I may, Congressman, I'd like to ask Dr. Haynes of the Bennett County Health Service to address that. Doctor?"

Dr. Haynes leaned into the microphone, "If I may, I'd like to provide some context on how Vectelon came to the reservation. What I've come to understand is that soon after the buildup of Middle East tensions, and, the conflicts with Iraq and Afghanistan, the DOD was looking closely at inoculating troops against biological weaponry. As a result, many thousands of U.S. troops were vaccinated as a preventive measure. And Vectelon promoted their ability to deliver certain products in response to this."

"What were these products?"

"They began by producing vaccines. Later, there were biological agents shipped overseas."

"Why were they being produced on the Manoaka reservation?

"Several reasons. According to governmental treaties dealing with bio-hazardous materials, certain experiments could not be conducted in government laboratories. As members of the Indian Affairs committee, I don't have to tell you ladies and gentlemen that a reservation such as the Manoaka Reservation is a sovereign state, not bound by international treaties that our government might have entered into with other countries. That was the main reason that Vectelon contracted with the tribe.

"After they began working with Vectelon, several tribe members came to our clinic for treatment.

They were experiencing a range of symptoms that took some time to identify. Even a well-trained physician might not recognize the effects of bio-toxins on the human body. The symptoms may be very different from the natural disease process caused by the same organism. Soon after exposure, the symptoms can feel like a cold coming on. There might be a sniffle and a cough. Then the cough gets worse, and it can lead to fatal pneumonia. After gaining more information, what I came to learn is that in the lab, they were working on biological toxins without the benefit of adequate safety measures or protective clothing."

"Can you be a little more specific?"

"The employees were working with infected lab animals. Two men died as a result of that exposure. These deaths, the result of negligence on the part of Vectelon, could have been avoided by following standard laboratory protocols."

"Dr. Haynes, how was this negligence allowed to occur?"

"From what I understand, proper laboratory guidelines were initially followed, but once the laboratory manager, Mr. Ricklin, left the facility, he was not replaced by adequately trained staff. There was a lot of pressure to deliver products in a tight time frame. During that period, adequate protective gear wasn't ordered. Safety procedures were ignored."

"Doctor, these are very strong charges. Can you provide proof of any of your statements?"

"Weaponized anthrax is made of anthrax spores dried into a powder and is sometimes converted into a liquid concentrate. We have evidence that this type of anthrax was shipped from this facility."

Cameras flashed from the front of the room. A buzz erupted in the spectator area. Sandi scanned the room. Getting up from her seat, she moved to a spot right behind Garrett. She was able to look over his shoulder as he opened a folder of what he called his "mug shots", the photos of

Vectelon's top management. "I didn't spot any of these guys," he whispered. "They probably sent the B-team, maybe even just their lawyers. Guess they didn't think they had much to worry about here."

With hands over microphones, the three additional Congressional committee members conferred looking like see no evil, and hear no evil. Sandi thought. The chairman struggled to regain control. He gaveled, "Order, order."

"What I don't understand is why they didn't call on those crooks from Vectelon and make them testify. Garrett, didn't that seem wrong to you?"

Garrett stopped fiddling with the car radio long enough to take the fake cigarette from between his lips. "If you want my opinion, Vectelon has got friends in high places."

"But Indian Affairs is a government agency."

"In Washington circles, Indian Affairs is like a throwback to ancient history. My guess is that if you dig a little, one committee member may sit on another committee where interests overlap. Don't forget that everybody in Congress is in bed with more than one person at a time."

Sandi sat silently, listening to the radio. As traffic slowed through northern Maryland, she was glad they were halfway back to Philadelphia, getting further from Washington, D.C. every minute. Even though her body felt slow with fatigue, her mind was racing. The last month was a blur of activity. It hadn't gotten off to a great start. When she got her grades back, her low second-year grade point average came as a shock, but it really shouldn't have. At best, her work for the second semester had been catch as catch can. If it weren't for Ned's help, him spoon-feeding her and propping up her contributions to the study group, she might not have passed two out of three of her courses. Thank goodness her grades from her first-year coursework were strong. At least, she had that to soften the blow, providing her with an overall GPA that would allow her to move on to her third year of law school.

"What are you doing this summer?" Garrett's voice broke into her thoughts.

"I'll be staying in the city. Working at the Vets Center. I'm going to be setting up a network so that vets around the country can communicate and keep in touch about the status of their claims against the government."

"That pay much?"

"Since you ask, the answer is no. But I'm doing it anyway, doing it for Joe."

"Just in case, I might have some work for you if you are interested. Work that pays."

Before Sandi could answer, the radio announcer's message pierced their consciousness. "And in today's financial news, Vectelon Corporation, headquartered in Washington, D.C. and facing legal jeopardy, was on the bloc."

Eyes wide, Garrett turned up the volume.

"After charges of criminal wrongdoing were made in front of a Congressional committee, the ailing company's stock plummeted drastically. As Wall Street buzzed with the news, defense contractor, Prodexo took advantage of Vectelon's bargain basement stock prices, scooping up a controlling interest before the market closed. In other news…"

Sandi and Garrett looked dumbstruck at each other. He flicked off the radio, hitting the gas as the traffic bottleneck seemed to open up after the gawkers finally got their chance to inch past a three-car pile-up on the shoulder.

Mark Ricklin, in an orange jumpsuit, made the rounds of the prison exercise yard with another inmate. "So, they tell this Congressional committee that the company, Vectelon, is making products used for germ warfare and shipping them overseas. It was my case. I was ready to file a lawsuit. And what does it get me now? Nothing."

"Man, I hear you. It was a setup."

"I was framed and I can prove it," Ricklin said.

"Yeah, man. Me too."

As they passed by deserted cubicles and workstations, two security guards escorted Ken Daly from behind his desk, leading him toward the elevator. In the hallway, Daly made a quick turn in an effort to head back to his office. "This is outrageous. I need my files…my computer."

"Our orders are to escort you off the premises. Any personal effects will be sent to your home."

Two days later, a brown UPS truck drove slowly down a leafy street in suburban Maryland and stopped in front of a two-story brick colonial. The uniformed driver got out, moving around to the rear of the vehicle. He soon emerged pushing a hand truck, and headed to the front door. At the sound of the bell, Ken Daly appeared.

"Mr. Daly? Package for you."

"You wanna bring it in here."

The driver tipped the hand truck up over the ledge and into the hallway. He held out a clipboard. "Sign on line 24 please."

Daly took the pen, then looked up surprised from the clipboard to face a gun. The driver shot point blank.

CHAPTER
25

Sandi's footsteps echoed on the stone floor as she hurried down the corridor to the open door. As she entered the ward of the Veteran's Hospital, beds lined both sides of the long room. Young men in various stages of recovery called out for her attention.

"Sandi. Don't forget. You were going to bring me the video."

"I told you I'd bring it. Here it is. You're gonna love it."

From the next bed, "Sandi, thanks for the birthday card. I got a kick out of it."

"Kevin, glad it gave you a chuckle. You are gonna have to tell me your beauty secret. I can't believe you turned twenty-nine."

After Sandi took a full turn around the room, speaking with every patient, a nurse entered. "Message for you. He's waiting out front."

Sandi waved her goodbyes as she headed to the elevator.

Outside, a black Jeep pulled to the entrance. She stepped forward and got inside. "Garrett, you should have come in with me. Tex is doing a lot better and the guys enjoy seeing you."

ABOUT THE AUTHOR

Arriving in Philadelphia as a college student, Lee Fishman fell in love with city living. Settling in, she soon came to value the cultural diversity and richness that would later provide the inspiration for her novels.

Recently retired from a satisfying career as assistant director at the Free Library of Philadelphia, she divides her time between writing and counseling women looking to re-enter the workforce. With a BA from Temple University and an MS from Drexel's School of Information, Lee supports free access to information for all people. She lives in Center City Philadelphia with her husband.

OTHER BOOKS BY THE AUTHOR

Edge of a Dream. Barely escaping the war-torn city of Sarajevo, Rija and Josef arrive in America hoping for a better life. When Josef, lured by dreams of easy money takes off for Las Vegas, Rija must find a way for herself and her young daughter to survive.

Mediums Guild. Margo often takes her psychic gifts for granted. When a young pilot asks for help to find a missing family member, Margo comes up short until a dream changes everything.

The Shaman's Gift. Carrie, a young scientist, travels to the Central American country of Belize to study with Don Rodrigo, a shaman who still practices the old ways. In this ecological thriller, Carrie is on a crusade to prevent the exploitation of the rainforest and its people for profit.

Follow on Instagram @leefishman01
On X@leefishman1
www.leefishman.net